FÜN學

美國英語閱讀課本 2
各學科實用課文 二版

+ **Workbook**

MP3

寂天雲 APP

AMERICAN
SCHOOL
TEXTBOOK
READING KEY

作者 Michael A. Putlack & e-Creative Contents　　譯者 丁宥暄

如何下載 MP3 音檔

❶ 寂天雲 APP 聆聽：掃描書上 QR Code 下載「寂天雲－英日語學習隨身聽」APP。加入會員後，用 APP 內建掃描器再次掃描書上 QR Code，即可使用 APP 聆聽音檔。

❷ 官網下載音檔：請上「寂天閱讀網」（www.icosmos.com.tw），註冊會員／登入後，搜尋本書，進入本書頁面，點選「MP3 下載」下載音檔，存於電腦等其他播放器聆聽使用。

American School Textbook
Reading Key

The Best Preparation for Building Academic Reading Skills and Vocabulary

The Reading Key series is designed to help students to understand American school textbooks and to develop background knowledge in a wide variety of academic topics. This series also provides learners with the opportunity to enhance their reading comprehension skills and vocabulary, which will assist them when they take various English exams.

Reading Key <Volume 1-3> is
a three-book series designed for beginner to intermediate learners.

Reading Key <Volume 4-6> is
a three-book series designed for intermediate to high-intermediate learners.

Reading Key <Volume 7-9> is
a three-book series designed for high-intermediate learners.

Features

- A wide variety of topics that cover American school subjects
  helps learners expand their knowledge of academic topics through interdisciplinary studies

- Intensive practice for reading skill development
  helps learners prepare for various English exams

- Building vocabulary by school subjects and themed texts
  helps learners expand their vocabulary and reading skills in each subject

- Graphic organizers for each passage
  show the structure of the passage and help to build summary skills

- Captivating pictures and illustrations related to the topics
  help learners gain a broader understanding of the topics and key concepts

Table of Contents

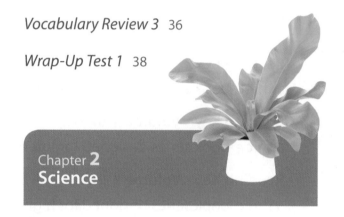

Chapter 2
Science

Workbook for Daily Review

Syllabus Vol. 2

Subject	Topic & Area	Title
Social Studies ★ **History and Geography**	Citizenship	Building Citizenship
	Citizenship	Different Kinds of Communities
	Government	The Leaders of Government
	Government	Martin Luther King, Jr.
	Economics	Many Jobs
	Economics	Volunteers and Community Jobs
	Geography	What Is a Map?
	Geography	Maps and Directions
	Geography	Natural Resources
	Geography	Caring for Our Resources
	American History	Native Americans
	American History	Early American Empires
Science	A World of Living Things	What Are Living Things?
	A World of Living Things	How Do Living Things Survive in the Cold?
	Plants	How Do Plants Grow and Change?
	Plants	How Do Plants Survive in the Desert?
	Animals	Kinds of Animals
	Animals	Insects
	The Life Cycle	The Life Cycle of an Animal
	The Life Cycle	The Life Cycle of a Frog
	The Food Chain	What Are Food Chains?
	The Food Chain	The Ocean Food Chain
	The Solar System	What Is the Solar System?
	The Solar System	What Causes the Seasons?
Mathematics	Computation	Addition and Subtraction
	Computation	Counting Money
	Time	Telling Time
	Time	Reading a Calendar
Language and Literature	Language Arts	Parts of Speech
	Language Arts	Contractions and Abbreviations
	Types of Writing	Types of Writing
	Reading Stories	The Emperor's New Clothes
Visual Arts	Visual Arts	A World of Colors
	Visual Arts	Lines and Shapes
Music	A World of Music	Musicians and Their Instruments
	A World of Music	Mozart and Beethoven

1

- **Social Studies**
- **History and Geography**

Building Citizenship

Key Words

- citizenship
- caring
- responsibility
- honesty
- courage
- fairness
- respect
- loyalty
- truth

We live together in a community.

How can you be a better citizen in your community?

There are seven ways to show good citizenship: caring, responsibility, honesty, courage, fairness, respect, and loyalty.

Caring means thinking about what others need.

Good citizens look after their neighbors and care for others.

Responsibility means doing the things you should do.

Always try to be a responsible person.

Good citizens should be honest.

Honesty means telling the truth.

It is not always easy to do the right thing.

That is why a good citizen needs courage, too.

Courage means being brave even when it is hard.

Good citizens treat others fairly and with respect.

Finally, good citizens are loyal to their friends, family, community, and country.

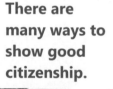

There are many ways to show good citizenship.

caring

responsibility

honesty

fairness

respect and loyalty

courage

Main Idea and Details

1 **What is the main idea of the passage?**

   a. People live together in communities.

   b. A good citizen should always be loyal.

   c. There are many ways to show good citizenship.

2 **A _____ person does the things he or she is supposed to do.**

   a. responsible   **b.** brave   **c.** loyal

3 **What does an honest person do?**

   a. Tell the truth.   **b.** Have courage.   **c.** Care for others.

4 **Complete the sentences.**

   a. Citizens live together in a _____.

   b. A _____ person has a lot of courage.

   c. People should _____ each other with respect.

5 **Complete the outline.**

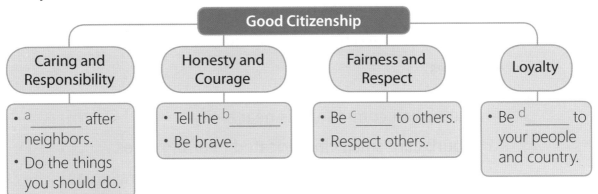

Vocabulary Builder

Write the correct word and the meaning in Chinese.

 ▸ the rights and responsibilities that a citizen has

_____

 ▸ treating people in a way that does not favor some over others

_____

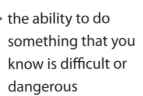 ▸ the ability to do something that you know is difficult or dangerous

_____

 ▸ being loyal to one's friends, community, and country

_____

Different Kinds of Communities

 02

There are many different kinds of communities.
Some communities are small, and others are big.

Key Words

- community
- urban
- apartment
- rural
- countryside
- be surrounded
- population
- be located
- suburban
- combination

An urban community is in a city.
Many people live and work in cities.
People in cities often live in big apartment buildings.
Supermarkets, department stores, and other stores are near their homes.

A rural community is in the countryside.
Usually, rural areas are surrounded by land and fields.
They have small populations.
People in rural areas usually live in houses.
Shops and buildings are often located far away from people's homes.

A suburban community is near a city.
Suburbs are small cities located near big cities.
They are like a combination of urban and rural areas.
Most suburbs are not as busy as cities.
They have medium-sized populations.

✔ There are many different kinds of communities.

urban community

rural community

suburban community

Main Idea and Details

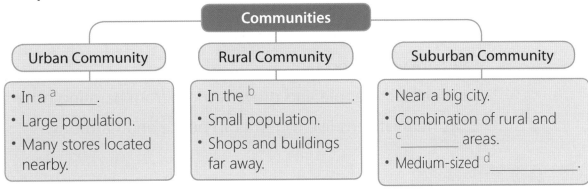

1 **What is the main idea of the passage?**

a. Rural communities are in the countryside.

b. People live in many different places.

c. Suburban places are small cities.

2 **What is in an urban area?**

a. Fields.

b. Suburbs.

c. Department stores.

3 **What does combination mean?**

a. Population.

b. Mix.

c. City.

4 **According to the passage, which statement is true?**

a. There are big apartment buildings in rural areas.

b. Suburban communities are large cities.

c. Urban communities have the largest populations.

5 **Complete the outline.**

Communities

Urban Community	Rural Community	Suburban Community
• In a ᵃ_____. • Large population. • Many stores located nearby.	• In the ᵇ_____. • Small population. • Shops and buildings far away.	• Near a big city. • Combination of rural and ᶜ_____ areas. • Medium-sized ᵈ_____.

Vocabulary Builder

Write the correct word and the meaning in Chinese.

1  ▸ of or relating to cities and the people who live in them

_____

2  ▸ the number of people who live in a place

_____

3  ▸ to be encircled by

_____

4  ▸ relating to country areas

_____

03

In the United States, each community and state has a leader.
People choose their leaders.

Key Words

- leader
- mayor
- vote
- governor
- president
- whole
- elect
- provide
- needs
- safety
- transportation

In a community, the mayor is the leader.
The citizens of the community vote for their leaders.
In a state, the governor is the leader.
The citizens of each state vote for their governor.
The president leads the whole country.
Every four years, the citizens elect a president to run the country.

The leaders provide for the needs of the people in the community, state, and country.
Some of these needs include education, safety, and transportation.
Each of these leaders also makes sure that people follow the law.
Laws are very important.
Laws protect people and prevent them from harming others.
Laws help citizens live together in peace and harmony.

✓ What do leaders do?

Leaders make sure people follow the laws.

safety POLICE

911

Leaders provide for the needs of the community.

education

public transportation

Main Idea and Details

1 **What is the main idea of the passage?**

a. The president is more important than a mayor.

b. Leaders take care of people in their communities.

c. There are many leaders in the United States.

2 **A _____ is the leader of a state.**

a. president   b. mayor   c. governor

3 **What do laws do?**

a. Decide who becomes the president.

b. Let people live together peacefully.

c. Provide for needs like transportation.

4 **Answer the questions.**

a. Who is the leader of the whole country? _____

b. Who chooses leaders? _____

c. What are some needs of the people? _____

5 **Complete the outline.**

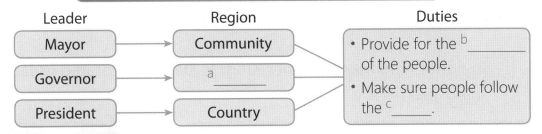

Leaders take care of people in their communities.

Leader	Region	Duties
Mayor	Community	• Provide for the b_____ of the people.
Governor	a _____	• Make sure people follow the c _____.
President	Country	

Vocabulary Builder

Write the correct word and the meaning in Chinese.

1 ▸ the leader of a community

_____

2 ▸ something that a person must have

_____

3 ▸ freedom from danger

_____

4 ▸ a system or means of moving people or goods

_____

04

Martin Luther King, Jr. was a great leader.

He grew up in the American South in the middle of the 1900s.

He was a black man.

At that time, many Americans treated blacks very poorly.

Dr. King believed that all people should have the right to be treated the same.

He dreamed for all people to live together in peace.

He led marches and gave speeches.

He was arrested many times, but he never gave up.

He believed in nonviolence.

In 1964, he won the Nobel Peace Prize.

That same year, the United States passed the Civil Rights Act.

It changed the laws that were unfair to African-Americans.

It guaranteed equal rights to all Americans.

To honor him, Martin Luther King, Jr. Day is celebrated in January every year.

Key Words
- grow up
- peace
- march
- speech
- arrest
- give up
- peace
- nonviolence
- Civil Rights Act
- law
- African-American

✔ **Dr. King wanted fair treatment for African-Americans.**

He gave the famous "I have a dream" speech in front of the Lincoln Memorial.

I have a dream today!

Main Idea and Details

1 What is the passage mainly about?
a. Martin Luther King, Jr.
b. The Nobel Peace Prize.
c. The Civil Rights Act.

2 What did Martin Luther King, Jr. believe in?
a. Nonviolence.　　　　**b.** Unfairness.　　　　**c.** War.

3 What does guaranteed mean?
a. Passed.　　　　**b.** Asked for.　　　　**c.** Promised.

4 Complete the sentences.
a. Martin Luther King, Jr. lived in the _____ in the United States.
b. The police _____ Martin Luther King Jr. many times.
c. The _____ _____ Act was passed in 1964.

5 Complete the outline.

Martin Luther King, Jr.

Beliefs	Actions	Martin Luther King, Jr. Day
• All people should be ^a_____ the same. • All people should live together in peace.	• Led marches. • Gave ^b_____. • Helped get the Civil Rights Act passed.	• Is celebrated in ^c_____ every year. • Honors Martin Luther King, Jr.

Vocabulary Builder

Write the correct word and the meaning in Chinese.

 **1** ▸ to use the power of the law to take and keep

_____

 **2** ▸ to abandon; to stop doing something

_____

 **3** ▸ the practice of refusing to respond to anything with violence

_____

 **4** ▸ an act that guaranteed equal rights to all Americans

_____

A Complete the sentences with the words below.

| loyal | fairly | countryside | honesty |
| suburban | city | responsibility | located |

1 Good citizens treat others _____ and with respect.

2 _____ means doing the things you should do.

3 _____ means telling the truth.

4 Good citizens are _____ to their friends, family, community, and country.

5 An urban community is in a _____.

6 A rural community is in the _____.

7 In rural areas, shops and buildings are often _____ far away from people's homes.

8 A _____ community is near a city.

B Complete the sentences with the words below.

| governor | prevent | vote | elect |
| guaranteed | unfair | poorly | right |

1 The citizens of the community _____ for their leaders.

2 In a state, the _____ is the leader.

3 Every four years, the citizens _____ a president to run the country.

4 Laws protect people and _____ them from harming others.

5 In the middle of the 1900s, many Americans treated blacks very _____.

6 Dr. King believed that all people should have the _____ to be treated the same.

7 The Civil Rights Act changed the laws that were _____ to African-Americans.

8 The Civil Rights Act _____ equal rights to all Americans.

C

Write the correct word and the meaning in Chinese.

1 ▸ the ability to do something that you know

_____

2 ▸ of or relating to cities and the people who live in

_____

3 ▸ relating to country areas

_____

4 ▸ the leader of a community

_____

5 ▸ a system or means of moving people or goods

_____

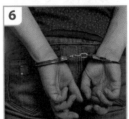
6 ▸ to use the power of the law to take and keep

_____

D

Match each word with the correct definition and write the meaning in Chinese.

1 citizenship _____ ☐

2 fairness _____ ☐

3 loyalty _____ ☐

4 population _____ ☐

5 be surrounded by _____ ☐

6 needs _____ ☐

7 safety _____ ☐

8 give up _____ ☐

9 nonviolence _____ ☐

10 Civil Rights Act _____ ☐

a. requirements

b. to be encircled by

c. freedom from danger

d. being fair and treating others fairly

e. to abandon; to stop doing something

f. the number of people living in a place

g. an act that guaranteed equal rights to all Americans

h. the rights and responsibilities that a citizen has

i. being loyal to one's friends, community, and country

j. not using violence; the practice of refraining from violence

05

Many people have jobs.

A job is the work that people do.

Most people work at a job to earn money.

They usually get paid hourly, weekly, or monthly.

With that money, they can take care of themselves and their families.

There are many kinds of jobs.

Some workers earn money by growing or making goods.

Farmers produce the food we eat every day.

Workers at factories produce many products we use every day.

Some workers earn money by having service jobs.

These are jobs like waiter, cook, delivery person, and salesperson.

Workers with these jobs provide services for others.

Others have professional jobs.

Professional jobs require special education and training.

Some of these jobs are doctor, lawyer, engineer, and artist.

Key Words

- job
- earn money
- get paid
- take care of
- grow
- goods
- produce
- factory
- service
- professional

✔ People work in many different places.

farmer

businessperson

factory worker

bus driver

waiter

doctor

18

Main Idea and Details

1 What is the passage mainly about?

a. The different jobs people have.

b. How much money some jobs pay.

c. Professional and service jobs.

2 Why do most people work?

a. To provide services for others.   b. To make goods.   c. To earn money.

3 What does goods mean?

a. Objects.   b. Products.   c. Services.

4 According to the passage, which statement is true?

a. Farmers often work at factories.

b. Cook is a kind of service job.

c. People only get paid monthly.

5 Complete the outline.

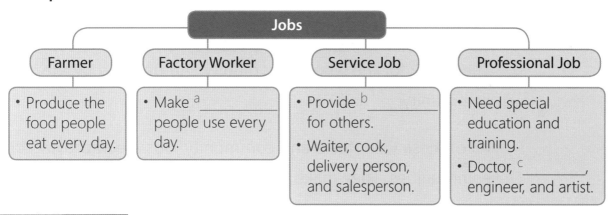

Jobs			
Farmer	**Factory Worker**	**Service Job**	**Professional Job**
• Produce the food people eat every day.	• Make ᵃ_____ people use every day.	• Provide ᵇ_____ for others. • Waiter, cook, delivery person, and salesperson.	• Need special education and training. • Doctor, ᶜ_____, engineer, and artist.

Vocabulary Builder

Write the correct word and the meaning in Chinese.

 **1** ▸ the work that a person does regularly in order to earn money

_____

 **2** ▸ to make money

_____

 **3** ▸ things that are grown or made; products

_____

 **4** ▸ work done by an organization or person that does not involve producing goods

_____

Key Words

- volunteer
- assist
- homeless shelter
- food bank
- unfortunate
- earthquake
- flood
- community job

Some people do not earn money for their work.
They work for free and help others.
We call them volunteers.

Volunteers do many important jobs.
Some people volunteer at hospitals.
They assist doctors and nurses in taking care of patients.
Other people work at homeless shelters or food banks.
They help take care of more unfortunate people.
Volunteers also help when people are in trouble because of earthquakes or floods.

There are also special jobs that help the whole community.
These are community jobs such as firefighter and police officer.
They work for the whole community and get paid by the community.

All of these volunteers and community jobs are improving our communities. They make our communities better places.

✓ Volunteers and community workers make a community a better place.

Main Idea and Details

1 **What is the main idea of the passage?**

   a. Firefighters help their communities.

   b. Volunteers do not make any money.

   c. Many people work to improve their communities.

2 **Who pays police officers?**

   a. The community.   **b.** Food banks.   **c.** Volunteers.

3 **What does unfortunate mean?**

   a. Unlucky.   **b.** Unhappy.   **c.** Unkind.

4 **Answer the questions.**

   a. How much money do volunteers earn? _____

   b. Where do some volunteers work? _____

   c. What are some community jobs? _____

5 **Complete the outline.**

> **Many people work to improve their communities.**

> **Volunteers**

> - Make no money.   • Help others.
> - Work at hospitals, homeless shelters, and ᵃ_____ _____.
> - Help after earthquakes and ᵇ_____.

> **Community Workers**

> - ᶜ_____ and police officers.
> - Work for the whole community.
> - Get paid by the ᵈ_____.

Vocabulary Builder

Write the correct word and the meaning in Chinese.

1  ▸ someone who does something without being forced to do it

_____

2  ▸ a temporary place provided for homeless people

_____

3  ▸ a sudden shaking of the earth's surface

_____

4  ▸ a large amount of water covering an area of land that is usually dry

_____

What Is a Map?

A map is a drawing of a place.

It looks like a view from above.

It might show cities, states, or countries.

It might show a small neighborhood or the entire world.

Key Words

• map
• view
• entire
• location
• symbol
• stand for
• map key
• title
• map feature

Maps can be very helpful.

Mostly, we use them to find locations.

We also use them to show how far one place is from another.

Most maps have symbols on them.

A symbol is a picture that stands for a real thing on a map.

There could be symbols for houses, buildings, rivers, mountains, streets, and more.

Maps have a map key.

A map key explains what the symbols on a map mean.

Maps also have titles.

The title tells you what the map shows.

These map features help us read and use the maps.

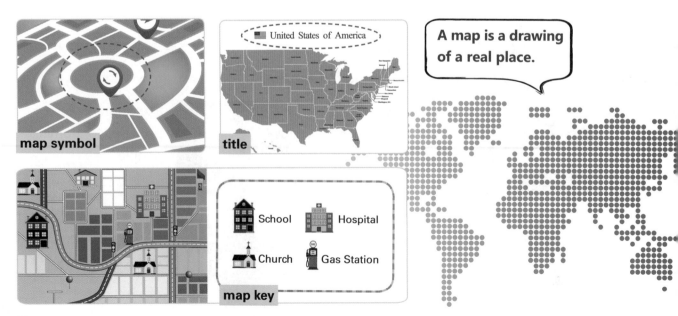

map symbol

title

United States of America

A map is a drawing of a real place.

School   Hospital

Church   Gas Station

map key

Main Idea and Details

1 **What is the passage mainly about?**

a. Who uses maps.

b. What maps look like.

c. How big maps are.

2 A _____ **explains the symbols on a map.**

a. location   b. map key   c. title

3 **What are the pictures that stand for real things on maps?**

a. Symbols.   b. Buildings.   c. Rivers.

4 **Complete the sentences.**

a. A map shows the view of something from _____.

b. A map can show the _____ of many places.

c. _____ _____, like the map key and title, help us read maps.

5 **Complete the outline.**

```
                              Maps

   What They Do              Symbols           Map Key and Title

 • Show ᵃ_____ from     • Are ᵇ_____     • Explain what the
   above.                  that stand for        ᶜ_____ mean.
 • Show locations.         real things.        • Tell what the map
 • Show how far one      • Can represent         shows.
   place is               houses,
   from another.          buildings, mountains, and
                          streets.
```

Vocabulary Builder

Write the correct word and the meaning in Chinese.

1 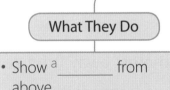 ▸ a drawing of a place or an area

_____

2  ▸ a place or position

_____

3 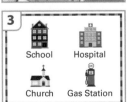 ▸ a table of symbols that shows what the symbols on a map mean

_____

4  ▸ to have (a specified meaning)

_____

Maps and Directions

Before we can use a map, we need to learn a few things about it.
First, we should find the compass rose.
The compass rose shows the four main directions on a map.
It points out which directions are north, south, east, and west.
On most maps, north is straight up on the map and is marked with an "N."
East is to the right, south is straight down, and west is to the left.

Maps also have a scale.
All maps are smaller than the real area that they show.
The map scale lets you calculate the real distance between two points.
For example, the scale on one map may be that one centimeter represents ten kilometers.
On this map, two cities are three centimeters away from each other.
In reality, thirty kilometers is the distance between the two cities.

Key Words

- compass rose
- direction
- point out
- mark
- scale
- calculate
- distance
- centimeter
- represent

✔ Four Main Directions

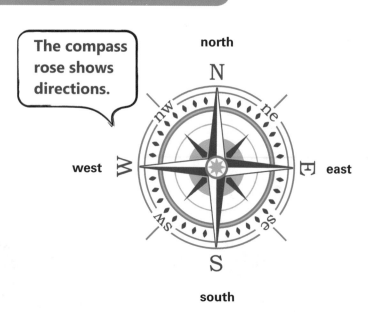

The compass rose shows directions.

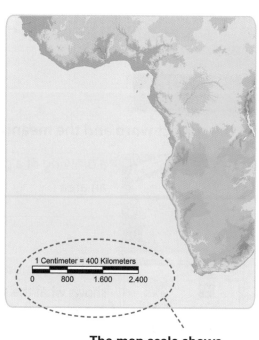

The map scale shows the real distance.

24

Main Idea and Details

1   What is the main idea of the passage?

a. The compass rose shows directions.

b. All maps have a compass rose and a scale.

c. Maps are not as big as the area they show.

2   Where is north on most maps?

a. Straight up.   b. Straight down.   c. To the right.

3   What does points out mean?

a. Answers.   b. Finds.   c. Shows.

4   According to the passage, which statement is true?

a. The compass rose lets you calculate the distance between two points.

b. The scale on all maps is one centimeter represents ten kilometers.

c. East is to the right on most maps.

5   Complete the outline.

How to Use Maps

Compass Rose

- Shows directions.
- North is straight up. • South is straight ᵃ_____.
- East is to the right. • West is to the ᵇ_____.

Scale

- Shows the ᶜ_____ between two points.
- Is needed because maps are ᵈ_____ than the area they show.

Vocabulary Builder

Write the correct word and the meaning in Chinese.

▸ a small drawing on a map that shows the four main directions

_____

▸ the course or path on which something is moving or pointing

_____

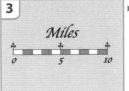
▸ It helps you calculate the actual distance between two places.

_____

▸ to be a sign or symbol of (someone or something)

_____

Vocabulary ▸ Review 2

A Complete the sentences with the words below.

> food banks   get paid   earn   growing
> police officer   professional   free   community

1 Most people work at a job to _____ money.

2 People usually _____ _____ hourly, weekly, or monthly.

3 Some workers earn money by _____ or making goods.

4 _____ jobs require special education and training.

5 Volunteers work for _____ and help others.

6 Volunteers work at homeless shelters or _____ _____.

7 There are also special jobs that help the whole _____.

8 These are community jobs such as firefighter and _____ _____.

B Complete the sentences with the words below.

> directions   marked   distance   features
> real area   symbols   drawing   locations

1 A map is a _____ of a place.

2 Mostly, we use maps to find _____.

3 A map key explains what the _____ on a map mean.

4 Map _____ help us read and use maps.

5 The compass rose shows the four main _____ on the map.

6 On most maps, north is straight up on the map and is _____ with an "N."

7 All maps are smaller than the _____ _____ that they show.

8 The map scale lets you calculate the real _____ between two points.

C Write the correct word and the meaning in Chinese.

1 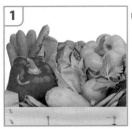 ▸ things that are grown or made; products

_____

2  ▸ someone who does something without being forced to do it

_____

3  ▸ a large amount of water covering an area of land that is usually dry

_____

4 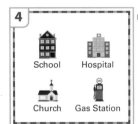 ▸ a table of symbols that shows what the symbols on a map mean

_____

5 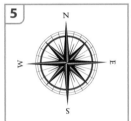 ▸ a small drawing on a map that shows the four main directions

_____

6  ▸ to have (a specified meaning)

_____

D Match each word with the correct definition and write the meaning in Chinese.

1 job _____ ☐

2 earn money _____ ☐

3 service _____ ☐

4 homeless shelter _____ ☐

5 earthquake _____ ☐

6 map _____ ☐

7 location _____ ☐

8 direction _____ ☐

9 map scale _____ ☐

10 represent _____ ☐

a. to show; to mean

b. the work that people do

c. a particular place or position

d. to make money

e. north, south, east, or west

f. a job people do to help others

g. a drawing of a place or an area

h. a sudden shaking of the earth's surface

i. a temporary place provided for homeless people

j. It helps you calculate the actual distance between two places.

Natural Resources

 09

Natural resources are useful things that come from nature.
Nature is full of resources that are ready for people to use.
Land, water, and air are some important natural resources.

We use natural resources for food and energy.
We need water to drink and air to breathe.
We need land and soil to grow food.
Coal, oil, and natural gas are used to make energy.
This energy lets us drive our cars and make electricity for our homes.

We also make many things from natural resources.
We can use cotton and wool from animals to make clothes.
We use trees to build our homes and to make many things we use every day.
Rocks can be used to build walls and buildings.

Key Words

- natural resources
- useful
- be ready
- energy
- breathe
- soil
- electricity
- cotton

✔ Things Made from Natural Resources

We use wood to make things.

Cotton and wool are used to make clothes.

Rocks are used to build walls and buildings.

paper

furniture

house

clothes

gloves

wall

building

Main Idea and Details

1 **What is the main idea of the passage?**

   a. Natural resources are important to people.

   b. People need air in order to breathe.

   c. We can make many things from natural resources.

2 **Coal, _____, and natural gas are used to make electricity.**

   a. soil   **b.** air   **c.** oil

3 **What do people use rocks for?**

   a. To make buildings.   **b.** To grow food.   **c.** To make clothes.

4 **Answer the questions.**

   a. Where can we find natural resources? _____

   b. What do we need to drink? _____

   c. What do we use to make clothes? _____

5 **Complete the outline.**

We use natural resources.

To Live	To Make Energy	To Make Things

- Food to eat.
- Water to drink
- Air to a_____.

- b_____, oil, and natural gas to make energy.

- Cotton and wool to make c_____.
- Trees to build homes and other things
- Rocks to make walls and buildings.

Vocabulary Builder

Write the correct word and the meaning in Chinese.

1 ▸ some useful things that come from nature

_____

2 ▸ usable power that comes from heat, electricity, etc.

_____

3 ▸ a form of energy that gives machines power to work

_____

4 ▸ to be prepared

_____

Caring for Our Resources

Key Words

- use up
- conserve
- reuse
- less
- reduce
- turn off
- recycle
- material
- recycling bin

We use natural resources every day.

So we have to be careful not to use up all of them.

If we do not save our natural resources, we might not have enough of them in the future.

One way to conserve resources is to reuse them.

Reuse paper, bags, and boxes as much as you can.

Another way to save resources is to use less of them.

Try to reduce the amount of resources you use.

You can turn off the lights when you leave a room.

You can turn the water off when you brush your teeth.

You can also recycle some materials.

To recycle means to make a new thing from an old thing.

Collect the used items and put them into the recycling bin.

When we recycle something, we can use it again and again.

We can conserve our natural resources!

The 3 R's for Saving Resources

Reduce, Reuse and Recycle

Please Recycle!

ORGANIC

PLASTIC

PAPER

GLASS

METAL

E-WASTE

MIXED

Main Idea and Details

1 What is the passage mainly about?

a. Which items we can recycle.

b. How to save our natural resources.

c. Where to put recycled items.

2 How can we reduce the resources we use?

a. Turn off the lights when we leave rooms.

b. Brush our teeth more often.

c. Buy many new products.

3 What does use up mean?

a. Order.   b. Buy.   c. Consume.

4 Complete the sentences.

a. We can _____ natural resources by reusing them.

b. You should turn the water _____ while brushing your teeth.

c. Put old items into the _____ bin.

5 Complete the outline.

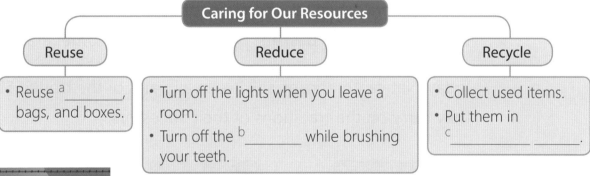

Caring for Our Resources

Reuse
- Reuse ᵃ_____, bags, and boxes.

Reduce
- Turn off the lights when you leave a room.
- Turn off the ᵇ_____ while brushing your teeth.

Recycle
- Collect used items.
- Put them in ᶜ_____ _____.

Vocabulary Builder

Write the correct word and the meaning in Chinese.

1 ▸ to keep (something) safe or from being damaged or destroyed

_____

2 ▸ to make (something) smaller in size, amount, number, etc.

_____

3 ▸ to switch off

_____

4 ▸ to treat used items so as to make them suitable to reuse

_____

Native Americans were the first people to live in America.
They are also called American Indians.

Key Words

- Native American
- American Indian
- ancestor
- tribe
- custom
- hunt
- craftwork
- carry on
- tradition

The ancestors of the Native Americans were people from Asia.
As the years passed, these people formed their own tribes.
They had their own languages and customs.
Some tribes hunted for their food.
Other tribes grew food such as corn and beans.

Native Americans lived in different types of homes.
The Lakota lived in tepees like tents.
The Pueblo lived in adobe houses.
The Iroquois lived in longhouses.

Native Americans made the things they used and wore.
They made canoes, baskets, pottery, and many other craftworks.

Today, Native Americans still live in all parts of the United States.
They carry on the traditions of their ancestors.

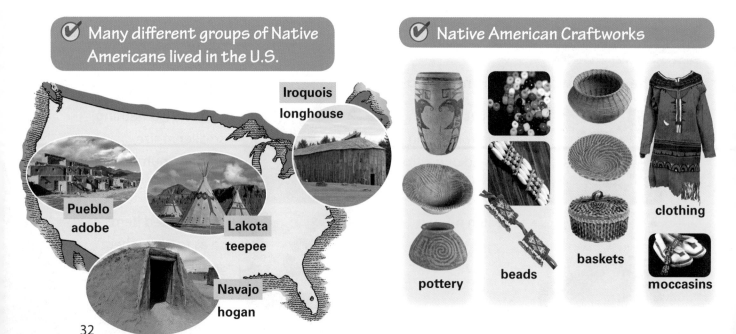

✔ Many different groups of Native Americans lived in the U.S.

Iroquois longhouse

Pueblo adobe

Lakota teepee

Navajo hogan

✔ Native American Craftworks

pottery

beads

baskets

clothing

moccasins

1 **What is the passage mainly about?**

    a. Native Americans and their customs.

    b. The things that Native Americans made.

    c. The homes of Native Americans.

2 **The Iroquois lived in** _____.

    a. adobe houses   **b.** longhouses   **c.** tepees

3 **What does carry on means?**

    a. Transport.   **b.** Hold on.   **c.** Continue.

4 **According to the passage, which statement is true?**

    a. There are no more Native Americans in the U.S.

    b. Native Americans made their own pottery.

    c. The Pueblo people lived in tepees.

5 **Complete the outline.**

Native Americans

Traditions
- Had their own languages and customs.
- Hunted for food.
- Grew ᵃ_____ like corn and beans.

Homes
- Lakota lived in tepees.
- Pueblo lived in. ᵇ_____ houses
- Iroquois lived in longhouses.

Customs
- Made canoes.
- Made baskets and pottery
- Made many ᶜ_____.
- Carry on ᵈ_____ of their ancestors today.

Write the correct word and the meaning in Chinese.

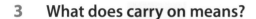 **1** ▸ the first people to live in America

_____

 **2** ▸ a person who was in someone's family in past times

_____

 **3** ▸ a group of people of the same race

_____

 **4** ▸ the way people do something because it is traditional

_____

There were many tribes in the Americas.

Some of them established their own empires.

The three great American empires were the Maya, Aztec, and Inca.

The Mayans lived in the jungles of Central America.

They built great cities with temples and palaces.

Their civilization was very developed.

The Mayans knew how to write.

They also had advanced math and building skills.

Like other ancient people, the Mayans worshipped many nature gods.

The Aztecs lived in the area of modern-day Mexico.

They built their city on islands in a lake.

The Aztecs were very warlike.

They conquered many people around them.

They built huge stone temples devoted to their sun god.

The Incas lived in the Andes Mountains in South America.

Their cities, like Machu Picchu, were high in the mountains.

The Incas built incredible stone walls.

Key Words

- establish
- empire
- Maya
- Aztec
- Inca
- temple
- palace
- civilization
- ancient
- worship
- nature god
- warlike
- conquer

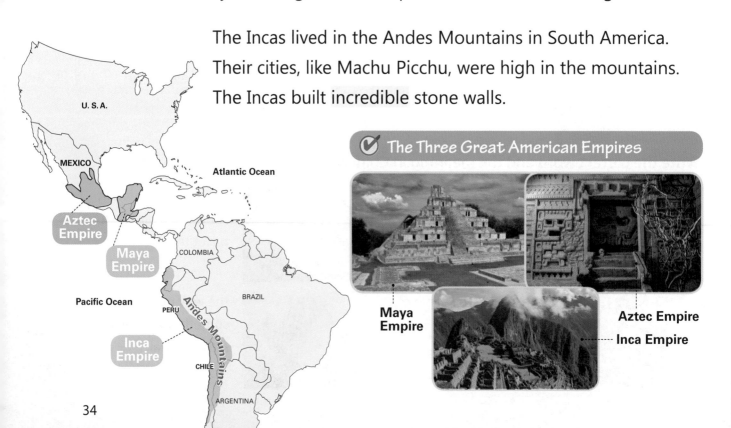

The Three Great American Empires

Maya Empire

Aztec Empire

Inca Empire

34

Main Idea and Details

1 **What is the main idea of the passage?**

  a. There were three great empires in America.

  b. The Mayans were greater than the Aztecs.

  c. The Incas lived in South America.

2 **Which empire was located in the jungle?**

  a. Inca.   **b.** Aztec.   **c.** Maya.

3 **What does incredible mean?**

  a. Tiny.   **b.** Great.   **c.** Pretty.

4 **Complete the sentences.**

  a. The Maya, Aztec, and Inca all established _____.

  b. The Aztecs were a _____ people.

  c. _____ _____ was one of the Inca's cities.

5 **Complete the outline.**

The Three Great American Empires

Maya Empire	Aztec Empire	Inca Empire
• Lived in the jungles of Central America. • Had advanced civilization. • Worshipped ª_____ _____.	• Lived in the area of modern-day ᵇ_____. • Were warlike. • Worshipped a sun god.	• Lived in the ᶜ_____ Mountains in South America. • One city was ᵈ_____ _____. • Built incredible walls.

Vocabulary Builder

Write the correct word and the meaning in Chinese.

 **1** ▸ a particular well-organized and developed society

_____

 **2** ▸ to show respect and honor for God or a god

_____

 **3** ▸ gods of the wind, rain, or sun

_____

 **4** ▸ liking or tending to fight in wars or to start wars

_____

A Complete the sentences with the words below.

less	reuse	energy	natural gas
useful	wool	recycle	use up

1 Natural resources are _____ things that come from nature.

2 We use natural resources for food and _____.

3 Coal, oil, and _____ _____ are used to make energy.

4 We can use cotton and _____ from animals to make clothes.

5 We have to be careful not to _____ _____ all of resources.

6 One way to conserve resources is to _____ them.

7 Another way to save resources is to use _____ of them.

8 To _____ means to make a new thing from an old thing.

B Complete the sentences with the words below.

homes	jungles	Inca	American Indians
tribes	ancestors	Andes	modern-day

1 Native Americans are also called _____ _____.

2 The _____ of the Native Americans were people from Asia.

3 Native American _____ had their own languages and customs.

4 Native Americans lived in different types of _____.

5 The three great American empires were the Maya, Aztec, and _____.

6 The Mayans lived in the _____ of Central America.

7 The Aztecs lived in the area of _____ Mexico.

8 The Incas lived in the _____ Mountains in South America.

Write the correct word and the meaning in Chinese.

1  ▸ some useful things that come from nature

_____

2  ▸ a form of energy that gives machines power to work

_____

3  ▸ to treat used items so as to make them suitable to reuse

_____

4  ▸ the first people to live in America

_____

5  ▸ gods of the wind, rain, or sun

_____

6  ▸ liking or tending to fight in wars or to start wars

_____

D

Match each word with the correct definition and write the meaning in Chinese.

1 energy _____ ☐

2 be ready _____ ☐

3 conserve _____ ☐

4 reduce _____ ☐

5 turn off _____ ☐

6 ancestor _____ ☐

7 tribe _____ ☐

8 custom _____ ☐

9 civilization _____ ☐

10 worship _____ ☐

a. to be prepared

b. to switch off

c. to use less

d. to save, keep, or protect

e. a group of people of the same race

f. an advanced state of human society

g. a family member who lived in the past

h. power that makes things work or change

i. to show respect and honor for God or a god

j. the way people do something because it is traditional

A Write the correct word for each sentence.

| natural resources | craftworks | leader | look after | off |
| Native Americans | populations | volunteers | worshipped | job |

1   Good citizens _____ _____ their neighbors and care for others.

2   Suburban communities have medium-sized _____.

3   In the United States, each community and state has a _____.

4   Most people work at a _____ to earn money.

5   _____ work for free and help others.

6   Land, water, and air are some important _____ _____.

7   You can turn the water _____ when you brush your teeth.

8   _____ _____ were the first people to live in America.

9   Native Americans made canoes, baskets, pottery, and many other _____.

10 Like other ancient people, the Mayans _____ many nature gods.

B Write the meanings of the words in Chinese.

1	courage	_____	16	homeless shelter	_____
2	urban	_____	17	location	_____
3	rural	_____	18	direction	_____
4	transportation	_____	19	map scale	_____
5	citizenship	_____	20	represent	_____
6	fairness	_____	21	natural resources	_____
7	loyalty	_____	22	electricity	_____
8	needs	_____	23	recycle	_____
9	give up	_____	24	conquer	_____
10	nonviolence	_____	25	be ready	_____
11	goods	_____	26	conserve	_____
12	flood	_____	27	reduce	_____
13	map key	_____	28	ancestor	_____
14	compass rose	_____	29	custom	_____
15	earn money	_____	30	civilization	_____

2

• Science

What Are Living Things?

Everything on Earth is either living or nonliving.
Animals and plants are living things.
Living things need food, water, and air to live.
Living things grow and change.
They can also make new living things like themselves.

Water, air, and rocks are nonliving things.
Nonliving things do not need food, water, or air.
Nonliving things do not grow or change.
They cannot make new things like themselves.

Living things must have shelter.
Shelter is a safe place to live.
Shelter protects them from their environment and from other animals.
Living things also must have room to grow or to move around.
Some living things, such as flowers, need very little space.
Other living things, such as elephants, may need a lot of space.

Key Words

- living
- nonliving
- plants
- shelter
- environment
- room
- move around
- space

✓ Living Things

✓ Nonliving Things

Main Idea and Details

1 **What is the main idea of the passage?**

a. Water and rocks are nonliving things.

b. Living things need food and shelter.

c. Everything is either living or nonliving.

2 **Living things need _____ for protection.**

a. air **b.** shelter **c.** water

3 **How much space does an elephant need?**

a. None. **b.** A little. **c.** A lot.

4 **Complete the sentences.**

a. All _____ things need food, air, and water to live.

b. Living things can make _____ living things like themselves.

c. _____ protects living things from their environment.

5 **Complete the outline.**

Everything on Earth

Living Things

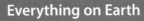

ª _____ and plants

- Need food, water, and air.
- Grow and change.
- Can make new ᵇ_____ _____.
- Need shelter and space.

Nonliving Things

Water, air, and rocks

- Do not need food, water, or air.
- Do not ᶜ_____ or change.
- Cannot make new things.

Vocabulary Builder

Write the correct word and the meaning in Chinese.

1  ▶ not dead : having life

_____

2  ▶ having no life; not living

_____

3  ▶ a structure that covers or protects people or things

_____

4  ▶ the land, water, and air in which living things live

_____

2

Science

How Do Living Things Survive in the Cold?

 14

The coldest place on Earth is Antarctica.

The temperature there is always below freezing.

But many animals still live there.

How do they manage to survive in such cold weather?

Key Words

- Antarctica
- below freezing
- manage to
- survive
- adapt
- layer
- fat
- think
- feather
- Arctic tundra
- fur

These animals have adapted their bodies to the cold.

Seals and whales in Antarctica have many layers of fat.

This fat helps keep their bodies warm.

Penguins stay warm because they have small and thick feathers.

Some plants and animals live in the Arctic tundra.

Many tundra animals have thick fur to keep them warm.

Plants do not grow very tall there.

They grow in groups close to the ground.

This protects them from the cold and the wind.

What about humans?

Clothing helps people stay warm the same way animals' fur does.

✔ How have plants and animals adapted to living in the cold?

Seals have many layers of fat.

Polar bears have thick fur and fat.

Arctic plants grow in groups close to the ground.

Main Idea and Details

1   What is the passage mainly about?

a. Why seals have lots of fat

b. Which plants can grow in the Arctic tundra

c. How animals and plants survive in cold places

2   What lets penguins stay warm in cold places?

a. Their feathers.   b. Their fat.   c. Their fur.

3   What does thick mean?

a. Heavy.   b. Fat.   c. Thin.

4   According to the passage, which statement is true?

a. No plants are able to grow in the Arctic tundra.

b. Clothing keeps people warm like fur does for animals.

c. Whales have thick fur to keep them warm.

5   Complete the outline.

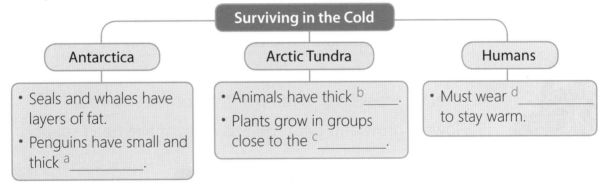

Surviving in the Cold

Antarctica
- Seals and whales have layers of fat.
- Penguins have small and thick [a]_____.

Arctic Tundra
- Animals have thick [b]_____.
- Plants grow in groups close to the [c]_____.

Humans
- Must wear [d]_____ to stay warm.

Vocabulary Builder

Write the correct word and the meaning in Chinese.

▸ to remain alive : to continue to live

_____

▸ to change something to fit a new environment

_____

▸ the continent surrounding the South Pole

_____

▸ of or relating to the North Pole or the region around it

_____

How Do Plants Grow and Change?

 Every living thing has a life cycle.

A life cycle shows how a living thing grows, lives, and dies.

A plant's life cycle begins with a seed.

When a seed gets water and nutrients from the soil, it starts to germinate.

Then, the seed sprouts and grows into an adult plant.

Again, the adult plant makes seeds, and a new life cycle begins.

Key Words

- life cycle
- seed
- nutrients
- germinate
- sprout
- plant
- water
- grow down
- seedling
- fertilize

The life cycle of a bean plant

Let's look closely at the life cycle of a bean plant.

1. A bean seed is planted and watered in the ground.

2. After around a week, the seed germinates. The roots grow down.

3. Then, one week later, the bean plant sprouts and becomes a seedling.

4. After six weeks, the bean plant becomes an adult.

5. Flowers grow and get fertilized. They make bean seeds.

seed

seed with roots
(germinate)

sprouting seed

seedling

adult bean plant

making seeds
(new cycle begins)

Main Idea and Details

1 **What is the passage mainly about?**

a. Plants' life cycles.

b. Seedlings.

c. How seeds germinate.

2 **A plant begins its life cycle as a _____ .**

a. flower   b. seed   c. seedling

3 **How long does it take a bean seedling to become an adult plant?**

a. One week.   b. Two weeks.   c. Six weeks.

4 **Answer the questions.**

a. What does a seed need to germinate?   _____

b. After a seed germinates, what happens?   _____

c. What makes bean seeds?   _____

5 **Complete the outline.**

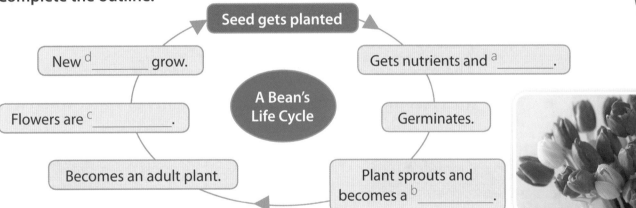

Seed gets planted

New ᵈ_____ grow.

Gets nutrients and ᵃ_____ .

A Bean's Life Cycle

Flowers are ᶜ_____ .

Germinates.

Becomes an adult plant.

Plant sprouts and becomes a ᵇ_____ .

Vocabulary Builder

Write the correct word and the meaning in Chinese.

1
▸ It shows how a living thing grows, lives, and dies.
_____

2
▸ a seed begin to grow
_____

3
▸ to send up new growth
_____

4
▸ a young plant that is grown from seed
_____

16

Key Words

- desert
- harsh
- dry
- cactus
- thick
- stem
- spiny leaf
- store
- spread out
- capture

Plants live almost everywhere.

Some plants even live in the desert.

Deserts have very harsh environments.

Deserts are very hot and dry with little rain.

Few kinds of plants and animals have adapted to living there.

However, some plants, like the cactus, grow well in the desert.

How do they manage to survive in such dry place?

A cactus has a thick stem and spiny leaves.

The stems and leaves help the cactus store water inside it.

Then, it can use the water later when it needs it.

So, it can grow for a long time without any rain at all.

A cactus's roots spread out away from it.

The roots are also very close to the ground.

This lets the roots capture large amounts of water when it rains.

✔ Cacti have adapted to living in the desert.

✔ A cactus's stem and leaves help store water.

Main Idea and Details

1 What is the main idea of the passage?

    a. A cactus needs little water to survive.

    b. Some plants can survive in harsh conditions.

    c. There are many cacti in the desert.

2 Which part of the cactus stores water?

    a. The stem.   **b.** The roots.   **c.** The branches.

3 What does capture mean?

    a. Use.   **b.** Drink.   **c.** Collect.

4 Complete the sentences.

    a. _____ are often very hot and dry.

    b. A cactus can store _____ to use another time.

    c. The _____ of a cactus spread out underground.

5 Complete the outline.

Cactus

Desert Environment	Stem and Leaves	Roots
• Very hot and dry. • Has ᵃ_____ to survive in the desert.	• Help ᵇ_____ water. • Can use the water when it is needed.	• Spread out away from it. • Close to the ᶜ_____. • Lets cactus ᵈ_____ water when it rains.

Vocabulary Builder

Write the correct word and the meaning in Chinese.

 **1** ▸ unpleasant and difficult to accept or experience

_____

 **2** ▸ covered with spines or long, sharp points

_____

 **3** ▸ to collect and put (something) into one location for future use

_____

 **4** ▸ to stretch out; to expand

_____

A Complete the sentences with the words below.

| nonliving things | environment | coldest | fur |
| living things | manage to | adapted | air |

1 Animals and plants are _____ _____.

2 Living things need food, water, and _____ to live.

3 Water, air, and rocks are _____ _____.

4 Shelter protects living things from their _____ and from other animals.

5 The _____ place on Earth is Antarctica.

6 How do the animals _____ _____ survive in such cold weather?

7 Animals in Antarctica have _____ their bodies to the cold.

8 Many tundra animals have thick _____ to keep them warm.

B Complete the sentences with the words below.

| nutrients | seed | away | thick |
| life cycle | harsh | fertilized | cactus |

1 A _____ _____ shows how a living thing grows, lives, and dies.

2 A plant's life cycle begins with a _____.

3 When a seed gets water and _____ from the soil, it starts to germinate.

4 Flowers grow and get _____. They make bean seeds.

5 Deserts have very _____ environments.

6 Some plants, like the _____, grow well in the desert.

7 A cactus has a _____ stem and spiny leaves.

8 A cactus's roots spread out _____ from it.

C Write the correct word and the meaning in Chinese.

1 ▸ not dead : having life

_____

2 ▸ having no life; not living

_____

3 ▸ a seed begin to grow

_____

4 ▸ a young plant that is grown from seed

_____

5 ▸ the continent surrounding the South Pole

_____

6 ▸ covered with spines or long, sharp points

_____

D Match each word with the correct definition and write the meaning in Chinese.

1 environment _____ ☐

2 shelter _____ ☐

3 survive _____ ☐

4 adapt _____ ☐

5 Arctic _____ ☐

6 sprout _____ ☐

7 life cycle _____ ☐

8 harsh _____ ☐

9 store _____ ☐

10 spread out _____ ☐

a. to stay alive

b. a safe place to live

c. to send up new growth

d. to stretch out; to expand

e. the area around the North Pole

f. very difficult to live in; very unkind

g. to keep or save something for future use

h. It shows how a living thing grows, lives, and dies.

i. the land, water, and air in which living things live

j. to change something to fit a new environment

49

Kinds of Animals

Key Words

- mammal
- fur
- give birth to
- young
- feed
- bird
- wing
- lay eggs
- hatch
- reptile
- amphibian
- fish

What do a cat, a lion, and a dolphin have in common?
They are all mammals.
A mammal is an animal with fur or hair.
Most mammals give birth to live young.
Mammals feed their young with milk from their mothers.

A bird is an animal that has a beak, feathers, wings, and legs.
Most birds can fly using their wings.
Birds lay eggs. Chicks hatch from the eggs.
Ducks, peacocks, and penguins are all birds.

A reptile is an animal that has dry skin covered with scales.
Most reptiles lay eggs and walk on four legs.
Snakes, turtles, and alligators are all reptiles.

An amphibian is an animal that lives on land and in water.
Most amphibians have smooth, wet skin and lay eggs.
Frogs and salamanders are amphibians.

Fish live under water.
Most fish have scales, fins, and gills.
They lay eggs. Angelfish and sharks are fish.

How are animals different?

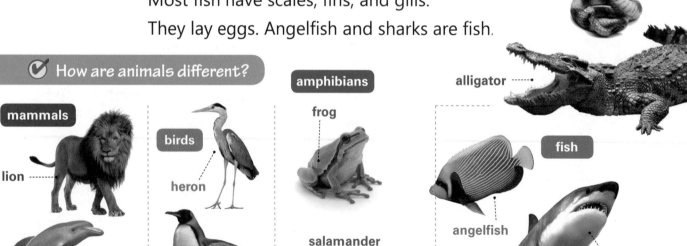

snake

reptiles

alligator

amphibians

frog

fish

mammals

lion

birds

heron

angelfish

shark

dolphin

penguin

salamander

Main Idea and Details

1 What is the passage mainly about?

a. The differences between reptiles and amphibians.

b. The environment that animals live in.

c. How animals are alike and different.

2 _____ can live both on land and in water.

a. Amphibians　　　　　**b.** Fish　　　　　　**c.** Mammals

3 What do many reptiles look like?

a. They have feathers.

b. They have skin covered with scales.

c. They have scales, fins, and gills.

4 According to the passage, which statement is true?

a. Birds feed their young milk from their mothers.

b. Reptiles lay eggs.

c. Dolphins are fish.

5 Complete the outline.

Kinds of Animals

Mammals	Birds	Reptiles	Amphibians	Fish
• Have fur or hair. • Give birth to live ᵃ_____. • Feed young milk from mothers.	• Have a beak, feathers, ᵇ_____, and legs. • Can fly. • Lay eggs.	• Have dry skin with ᶜ_____. • Lay eggs. • Walk on four legs.	• Live on land and in ᵈ_____. • Have smooth, wet skin.	• Live under water. • Have scales, fins, and ᵉ_____.

Vocabulary Builder

Write the correct word and the meaning in Chinese.

1

▸ a type of animal that feeds milk to its young

_____

2

▸ animals' babies

_____

3

▸ animals that live on land and in water

_____

4

▸ an animal that has cold blood, lays eggs, and has a body covered with scales or hard parts

_____

 There are millions of species of insects.
Insects include ants, butterflies, bees, and crickets.

Key Words

• species
• insect
• similarity
• lay
• head
• thorax
• abdomen
• antennae
• pair
• stinger

Many look different from one another.
But insects all have many similarities.
All insects have three body parts and six legs.
Most insects lay eggs.

Let's take a closer look at the three main body parts: the head, thorax, and abdomen.
The head has the insect's eyes, antennae, and mouth.
Insects use their antennae to feel things.
The thorax has the insect's legs and wings.
All insects have three pairs of legs.
Not all of them have wings though.
The abdomen is usually the largest part.
Female insects lay eggs from their abdomen.
Insects like bees have their stingers there.

☑ **The Three Parts of Insects**

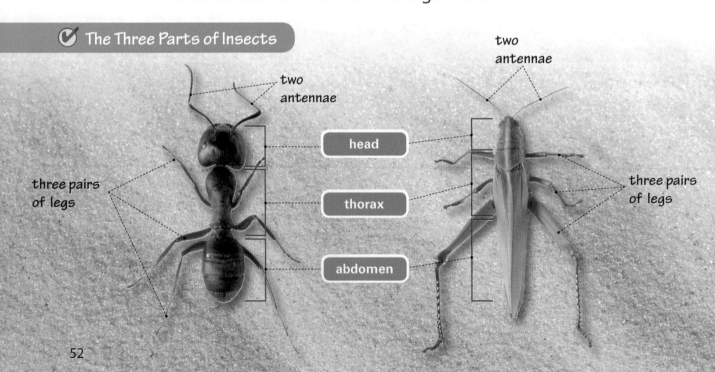

two antennae

two antennae

head

thorax

abdomen

three pairs of legs

three pairs of legs

Main Idea and Details

1   What is the passage mainly about?

a. Some species of insects.
b. The body parts of insects.
c. The wings and antennae of insects.

2   What do all insects have?

a. Six pairs of legs.   b. Wings.   c. Three body parts.

3   What does feel mean?

a. See.   b. Taste.   c. Touch.

4   Answer the questions.

a. What are the three body parts of an insect?   _____
b. What is on an insect's thorax?   _____
c. What do bees have on their abdomen?   _____

5   Complete the outline.

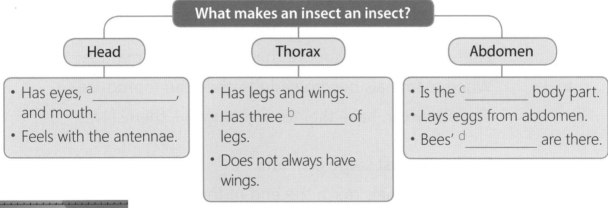

What makes an insect an insect?

Head	Thorax	Abdomen
• Has eyes, a_____, and mouth. • Feels with the antennae.	• Has legs and wings. • Has three b_____ of legs. • Does not always have wings.	• Is the c_____ body part. • Lays eggs from abdomen. • Bees' d_____ are there.

Vocabulary Builder

Write the correct word and the meaning in Chinese.

   ▸ the middle section of an insect's body

_____

   ▸ the largest body part of an insect, from which they lay eggs

_____

   ▸ two long things on an insect's head that it uses to feel with

_____

   ▸ a pointed part on an insect and animal that is used to sting someone

_____

The Life Cycle of an Animal

How do animals grow and change?

All animals have a life cycle.

A life cycle is all of the stages that animals go through during their lives.

Most animals go through four stages: birth, growth, reproduction, and death.

When mammals are born, they are helpless.

They cannot see or walk.

Their mothers must take care of them until they can take care of themselves.

As mammals grow up, they start to look like their parents.

For cats and dogs, it takes about a year to become an adult.

For humans, it takes more than ten years to mature.

When mammals become adults, they can reproduce.

Then they can have their own young like themselves.

Finally, the last stage is death.

When mammals reach the end of their lives, they die.

Key Words

- life cycle
- stage
- go through
- birth
- growth
- reproduction
- death
- helpless
- take care of
- mature
- reproduce
- reach
- end

✔ The Life Cycle of a Cat

| newborn cat | baby cat | young cat | adult cat |

Main Idea and Details

1   What is the passage mainly about?

a. The life cycles of mammals.

b. Cats and dogs growing older.

c. Mammals when they are born.

2   The third stage in a mammal's life cycle is _____.

a. death   b. reproduction   c. growth

3   How long does it take for dogs to mature?

a. One year.   b. Six years.   c. More than ten years.

4   Complete the sentences.

a. A life cycle is the _____ an animal goes through in its life.

b. Mammals are helpless at _____.

c. Mammals look like their _____ as they grow older.

5   Complete the outline.

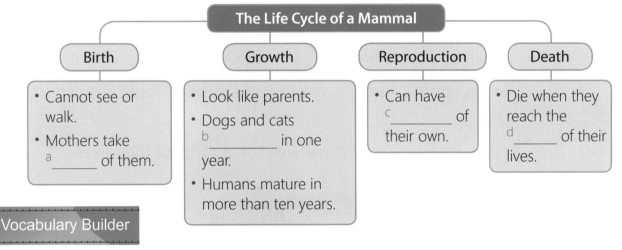

The Life Cycle of a Mammal

Birth
- Cannot see or walk.
- Mothers take ᵃ_____ of them.

Growth
- Look like parents.
- Dogs and cats ᵇ_____ in one year.
- Humans mature in more than ten years.

Reproduction
- Can have ᶜ_____ of their own.

Death
- Die when they reach the ᵈ_____ of their lives.

Vocabulary Builder

Write the correct word and the meaning in Chinese.

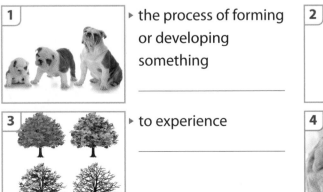 1 ▸ the process of forming or developing something

_____

2  ▸ the process that produces babies

_____

3 ▸ to experience

_____

4  ▸ to look after

_____

The Life Cycle of a Frog

Key Words

- amphibian
- unique
- lay eggs
- spring
- tadpole
- hatch
- resemble
- tail
- gills
- develop
- lungs

Frogs are amphibians.

So their life cycles are different from mammals.

In fact, frogs have very unique life cycles.

Frogs lay eggs in water in spring.

After about two weeks, tadpoles hatch from the eggs.

Tadpoles actually do not resemble frogs at all.

They do not have any legs but have tails.

Tadpoles also have gills.

Their gills let them breathe and live in the water.

As tadpoles grow older, they get ready to live on land.

They develop legs, and their tails become shorter.

Also, they develop lungs, which let them breathe air on land.

Then, the tadpoles start to look more like frogs.

After about 14 weeks, the frogs have become adults and have no tails.

They move onto land and live there most of their lives.

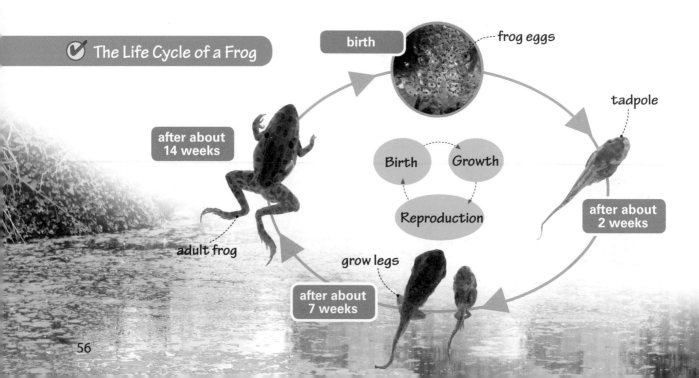

The Life Cycle of a Frog

birth — frog eggs

tadpole

after about 14 weeks

Birth   Growth

Reproduction

adult frog

grow legs

after about 2 weeks

after about 7 weeks

56

Main Idea and Details

1 **What is the main idea of the passage?**

a. A baby frog is called a tadpole.

b. Frogs can live in the water and on land.

c. The life cycle of a frog is unique.

2 **How can tadpoles breathe in the water?**

a. They have lungs.   **b.** They have gills.   **c.** They have tails.

3 **What does develop mean?**

a. Lose.   **b.** Grow.   **c.** Breathe.

4 **According to the passage, which statement is true?**

a. Tadpoles have both gills and lungs.

b. Tadpoles look like frogs.

c. Frogs are fully grown up after fourteen weeks.

5 **Complete the outline.**

```
                          Frogs
        ┌────────────────────┴────────────────────┐
     Tadpoles                                 Adult Frogs
```

Tadpoles	Adult Frogs
• Hatch from eggs. • Have a ᵃ_____ but no legs. • Have gills so can breathe in water. • Develop ᵇ_____ and lungs.	• Become adults after 14 weeks. • Have no tails. • Have legs and ᶜ_____ so can live on land.

Vocabulary Builder

Write the correct word and the meaning in Chinese.

1    ▸ a young frog

_____

2    ▸ to be born by coming out of an egg

_____

3    ▸ to look like something or someone

_____

4 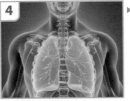   ▸ the two organs that people and animals use to breathe air

_____

Vocabulary Review 5

A

Complete the sentences with the words below.

give birth to	antennae	feed	common
lay eggs	species	legs	wings

1   What do a cat, a lion, and a dolphin have in _____?

2   Most mammals _____ _____ _____ live young.

3   Mammals _____ their young with milk from their mothers.

4   Most amphibians have smooth, wet skin and _____ _____.

5   There are millions of _____ of insects.

6   All insects have three body parts and six _____.

7   The head has the insect's eyes, _____, and mouth.

8   The thorax has the insect's legs and _____.

B

Complete the sentences with the words below.

helpless	reproduce	hatch	develop
change	grow older	stages	unique

1   How do animals grow and _____?

2   A life cycle is all of the _____ that animals go through during their lives.

3   When mammals are born, they are _____.

4   When mammals become adults, they can _____.

5   In fact, frogs have very _____ life cycles.

6   After about two weeks, tadpoles _____ from the eggs.

7   As tadpoles _____ _____, they get ready to live on land.

8   Tadpoles _____ legs, and their tails become shorter.

C
Write the correct word and the meaning in Chinese.

1 ▸ a type of animal that feeds milk to its young

_____

2 ▸ animals' babies

_____

3 ▸ animals that live on land and in water

_____

4 ▸ an animal that has cold blood, lays eggs, and has a body covered with scales or hard parts

_____

5 ▸ the middle section of an insect's body

_____

6 ▸ a young frog

_____

D
Match each word with the correct definition and write the meaning in Chinese.

1 abdomen _____ ☐

2 antennae _____ ☐

3 stinger _____ ☐

4 growth _____ ☐

5 reproduction _____ ☐

6 go through _____ ☐

7 take care of _____ ☐

8 hatch _____ ☐

9 resemble _____ ☐

10 lungs _____ ☐

a. to look after

b. to experience

c. to be born from an egg

d. the process of growing bigger

e. to look like something or someone

f. the act or process of having babies

g. a pair of body parts used for breathing air

h. the sharp stinging part of a bee that contains poison

i. two long things on an insect's head that it uses to feel things

j. the largest body part of an insect, from which they lay eggs

Key Words

- food chain
- energy
- order
- bottom
- link
- plant eater
- meat eater
- hunt

All animals need food to live.

Food gives them energy to survive.

Different animals eat different things.

Some eat plants. Some eat other animals.

A food chain shows the order in which animals eat plants and other animals.

At the bottom of the food chain are plants.

The sun gives plants energy.

Animals that eat plants are the next link.

We call them plant eaters.

They are usually small insects like grasshoppers.

Animals like squirrels and rabbits are also plant eaters.

Animals that eat other animals are the third link.

We call them meat eaters.

They might be small animals like frogs and snakes.

Then, bigger animals like hawks and bears eat these small animals.

Animals that are not hunted by other animals are at the top of the food chain. Actually, people are at the top of many food chains.

✓ Food Chain

Plants

Plant Eaters

Small Meat Eaters

Big Meat Eaters

Plant grows   **Insect eats the plant**   **Frog eats the insect**   **Snake eats the frog**   **Hawk eats the snake**

Main Idea and Details

1 **What is the passage mainly about?**

a. Different meat eaters.

b. The bottom of the food chain.

c. The links on the food chain.

2 _____ **are located at the bottom of the food chain.**

a. Plants

b. Insects

c. Frogs

3 **Which is a food chain?**

a. Plant → frog → rabbit → hawk.

b. Plant → grasshopper → frog → snake.

c. Snake → rabbit → bear → hawk.

4 **Answer the questions.**

a. Which animals are plant eaters? _____

b. Which animals are on the third link of the food chain? _____

c. Which animals are at the top of the food chain? _____

5 **Complete the outline.**

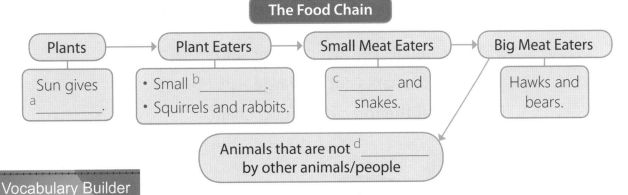

The Food Chain

Plants → Plant Eaters → Small Meat Eaters → Big Meat Eaters

Sun gives a_____.

• Small b_____.
• Squirrels and rabbits.

c_____ and snakes.

Hawks and bears.

Animals that are not d_____ by other animals/people

Vocabulary Builder

Write the correct word and the meaning in Chinese.

1  ▸ the order in which animals eat plants and other animals

_____

2  ▸ animals that eat other animals

_____

3  ▸ the way in which a set of things is arranged or done

_____

4  ▸ to connect things together so that they stay attached

_____

The Ocean Food Chain

Key Words

• exist
• life
• creature
• algae
• plankton
• consume
• shellfish
• shark
• killer whale

Food chains also exist in the oceans.

The oceans are full of life.

These life forms all either eat or get eaten by creatures on the food chain.

Algae are the lowest on the ocean food chain.

They are plants that make food from the sun's light.

Small creatures, such as plankton, consume the algae.

Then, slightly bigger creatures eat the plankton.

These are often shellfish like clams, shrimp, and crabs.

Then, small fish eat the shellfish.

Some small fish are cod, mackerel, and flatfish.

Next, large fish eat the small fish.

Some large fish are tuna, swordfish, and sharks.

Finally, animals like killer whales and great white sharks eat the large fish.

They are at the top of the food chain.

The Ocean Food Chain

Algae

Plankton eat algae

Shellfish eats plankton

Small fish eats shellfish

Large fish eats small fish

Killer whale eats large fish

Main Idea and Details

1   What is the main idea of the passage?

  a. There is a food chain in the ocean.

  b. Many small creatures eat plankton.

  c. Killer whales are at the top of the ocean food chain.

2   Which is the lowest on the ocean food chain?

  a. Shellfish.   **b.** Algae.   **c.** Plankton.

3   What does consume mean?

  a. Hunt.   **b.** Eat.   **c.** Chase.

4   Complete the sentences.

  a. Clams, shrimp, and crabs are all _____.

  b. _____ use the sun's light to make food.

  c. Great white sharks are at the _____ of the food chain.

5   Complete the outline.

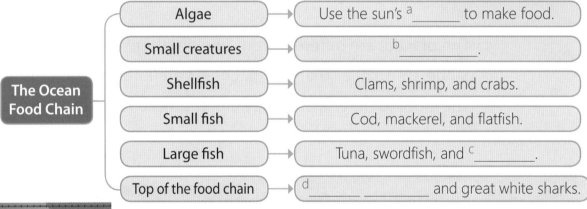

The Ocean Food Chain

Algae	→	Use the sun's ^{a}_____ to make food.
Small creatures	→	^{b}_____.
Shellfish	→	Clams, shrimp, and crabs.
Small fish	→	Cod, mackerel, and flatfish.
Large fish	→	Tuna, swordfish, and ^{c}_____.
Top of the food chain	→	^{d}_____ _____ and great white sharks.

Vocabulary Builder

Write the correct word and the meaning in Chinese.

 **1** ▸ simple plants that have no leaves or stems and that grow in or near water

_____

 **2** ▸ any living thing; life

_____

 **3** ▸ an animal that has a hard outer shell and that lives in water

_____

 **4** ▸ to eat or drink something; to use completely

_____

What Is the Solar System?

Key Words

- solar system
- be made up of
- planet
- object
- orbit
- path
- distance

We all live on Earth.

Earth is part of a larger system called the solar system.

The solar system is made up of the sun and the planets.

A planet is a huge object that moves around the sun.

There are eight planets in the solar system.

Earth is one of eight planets that orbit the sun.

In order of the planets from the sun, they are: Mercury, Venus, Earth, Mars, Jupiter, Saturn, Uranus, and Neptune.

The sun is the center of the solar system.

The eight planets move in paths around the sun.

Each path is called an orbit.

The planets are different from one another.

Some are smaller than Earth. Others are larger.

They look different, and they are at different distances from the sun.

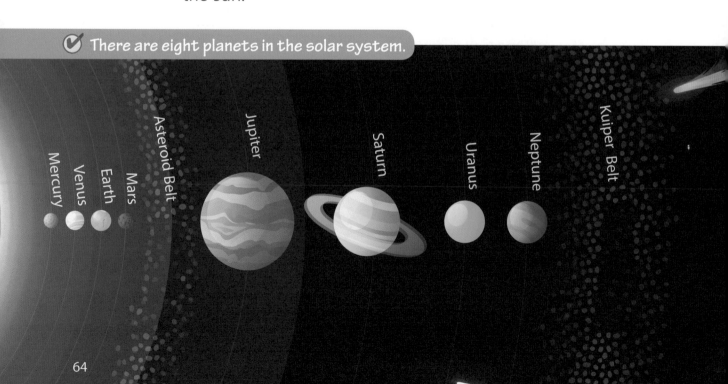

There are eight planets in the solar system.

Mercury Venus Earth Mars Asteroid Belt Jupiter Saturn Uranus Neptune Kuiper Belt

Main Idea and Details

1 **What is the passage mainly about?**

a. The characteristics of the planets.

b. The planets in the solar system.

c. The distance of the planets from the sun.

2 **The farthest planet from the sun is _____.**

a. Earth   b. Mercury   c. Neptune

3 **What does orbit mean?**

a. Fly.   b. Go through.   c. Move around.

4 **According to the passage, which statement is true?**

a. The planets all move around the sun.

b. Earth is the center of the solar system.

c. The planets all have the same size.

5 **Complete the outline.**

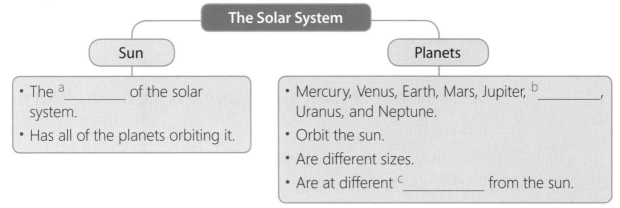

The Solar System

Sun

• The ᵃ_____ of the solar system.
• Has all of the planets orbiting it.

Planets

• Mercury, Venus, Earth, Mars, Jupiter, ᵇ_____, Uranus, and Neptune.
• Orbit the sun.
• Are different sizes.
• Are at different ᶜ_____ from the sun.

Vocabulary Builder

Write the correct word and the meaning in Chinese.

1 ▸ the sun and the planets

_____

2 ▸ a large, round object in space that travels around a star

_____

3 ▸ a track; a way that allows you to move forward

_____

4 ▸ the curved path that something follows as it goes around something else

_____

What Causes the Seasons?

Key Words

- season
- cause
- rotate
- complete
- full
- tilt
- direction
- sun's rays

There are four different seasons in a year: spring, summer, fall, and winter.

All throughout the year, the seasons change.

So what causes them to change?

Earth moves around the sun while it rotates each day.

It takes Earth one year to complete a full trip around the sun.

Earth is always tilted in the same direction.

As Earth orbits the sun, the part that is tilted toward the sun changes.

This makes the four seasons.

When the part of Earth where you live is tilted toward the sun, the sun's rays directly hit that part of Earth.

So it is summer.

When the part of Earth where you live is tilted away from the sun, it is winter.

The same pattern repeats each year.

✓ Earth is tilted as it moves around the sun.

Earth moves around the Sun.

spring

summer

winter

fall

Main Idea and Details

1   What is the main idea of the passage?

   a. The seasons change because of Earth's tilt.

   b. There are four seasons each year.

   c. The sun's rays hitting Earth directly make it summer.

2   How long does it take Earth to complete one orbit around the sun?

   a. One day.   **b.** One week.   **c.** One year.

3   What does is tilted mean?

   a. Changes.   **b.** Moves.   **c.** Leans.

4   Complete the sentences.

   a. The four _____ are spring, summer, fall, and winter.

   b. Earth is always tilted in the same _____.

   c. The part of Earth tilted away from the sun has _____.

5   Complete the outline.

```
                          Seasons
         ┌───────────────────┴───────────────────┐
   Four Seasons                          Why They Change

 Spring, summer,        • Earth is ᵇ_____ as it moves around the sun.
 ᵃ_____, and winter.   • The part tilted ᶜ_____ the sun has summer.
                        • The part tilted ᵈ_____ from the sun has
                          winter.
```

Vocabulary Builder

Write the correct word and the meaning in Chinese.

 1   ▸ to lift or move so that one side is higher than another side

_____

 2   ▸ to move or turn in a circle

_____

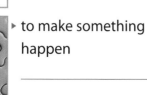 3   ▸ to make something happen

_____

 4   ▸ to finish doing something

_____

Vocabulary ▷ **Review 6**

A Complete the sentences with the words below.

plankton	plant eaters	animals	top
ocean	killer whales	plants	hunted

1 At the bottom of the food chain are _____.

2 Animals like squirrels and rabbits are _____ _____.

3 Animals that eat other _____ are the third link on the food chain.

4 Animals that are not _____ by other animals are at the top of the food chain.

5 Algae are the lowest on the _____ food chain.

6 Small creatures, such as _____, consume the algae.

7 Animals like _____ _____ and great white sharks eat the large fish.

8 People are at the _____ of many food chains.

B Complete the sentences with the words below.

Saturn	complete	throughout	system
direction	object	planets	away

1 Earth is part of a larger _____ called the solar system.

2 A planet is a huge _____ that moves around the sun.

3 In order of the planets from the sun, they are: Mercury, Venus, Earth, Mars, Jupiter, _____, Uranus, and Neptune.

4 The eight _____ move in paths around the sun.

5 All _____ the year, the seasons change.

6 It takes Earth one year to _____ a full trip around the sun.

7 Earth is always tilted in the same _____.

8 When the part of Earth where you live is tilted _____ from the sun, it is winter.

68

C Write the correct word and the meaning in Chinese.

1 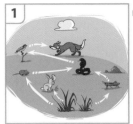 ▸ the order in which animals eat plants and other animals

_____

2  ▸ animals that eat other animals

_____

3  ▸ an animal that has a hard outer shell and that lives in water

_____

4  ▸ the sun and the planets

_____

5  ▸ to lift or move so that one side is higher than another side

_____

6  ▸ simple plants that have no leaves or stems and that grow in or near water

_____

D Match each word with the correct definition and write the meaning in Chinese.

1 order _____ ☐

2 link _____ ☐

3 creature _____ ☐

4 consume _____ ☐

5 planet _____ ☐

6 path _____ ☐

7 orbit _____ ☐

8 rotate _____ ☐

9 cause _____ ☐

10 complete _____ ☐

a. a ring of a chain

b. any living thing; life

c. a structure or system

d. to spin around or to turn

e. to finish doing something

f. to make something happen

g. to eat or drink something; to use completely

h. a large object that moves around the sun

i. a track; a way that allows you to move forward

j. the path traveled by a planet

Wrap-Up Test 2

Write the correct word for each sentence.

> stay warm   reptile   food chain   creatures   survive
> go through   nonliving   abdomen   seasons   planets

1   Everything on Earth is either living or _____.

2   Female insects lay eggs from their _____.

3   How do the animals manage to _____ in such cold weather?

4   Penguins _____ _____ because they have small and thick feathers.

5   A _____ is an animal that has dry skin covered with scales.

6   A life cycle is all of the stages that animals _____ _____ during their lives.

7   A _____ _____ shows the order in which animals eat plants and other animals.

8   Life forms all either eat or get eaten by _____ on the food chain.

9   The solar system is made up of the sun and the _____.

10   There are four different _____ in a year.

B

Write the meanings of the words in Chinese.

1	living	_____	16	hatch	_____
2	germinate	_____	17	resemble	_____
3	seedling	_____	18	food chain	_____
4	environment	_____	19	order	_____
5	shelter	_____	20	link	_____
6	adapt	_____	21	creature	_____
7	spread out	_____	22	consume	_____
8	mammal	_____	23	planet	_____
9	amphibian	_____	24	path	_____
10	reptile	_____	25	orbit	_____
11	abdomen	_____	26	rotate	_____
12	antennae	_____	27	cause	_____
13	stinger	_____	28	complete	_____
14	reproduction	_____	29	solar system	_____
15	take care of	_____	30	tilt	_____

3

- **Mathematics**
- **Language**
- **Visual Arts**
- **Music**

Addition and Subtraction

Addition is adding two or more numbers together.

Suppose there are 3 ants on a leaf. Then, 4 more ants join them.

How many ants are there now?

3 + 4 = 7

There are 7 ants.

The answer you get after you add numbers is called the *sum*.

So, you can say, "The sum of 3 + 4 is 7."

Or, you can say, "Three plus four equals seven."

Subtraction is taking a number away from another one.

Suppose your friend has 5 cookies.

You are hungry, so you take 2 cookies.

How many cookies are left now?

5 − 2 = 3

There are 3 cookies left.

The number you have left after you subtract is called the *difference*.

So, you can say, "The difference of 5 − 2 is 3."

Or, you can say, "Five minus two equals three."

Key Words

- addition
- add
- suppose
- join
- sum
- plus
- equals
- subtraction
- take away
- subtract
- difference
- minus

✓ Addition and Subtraction

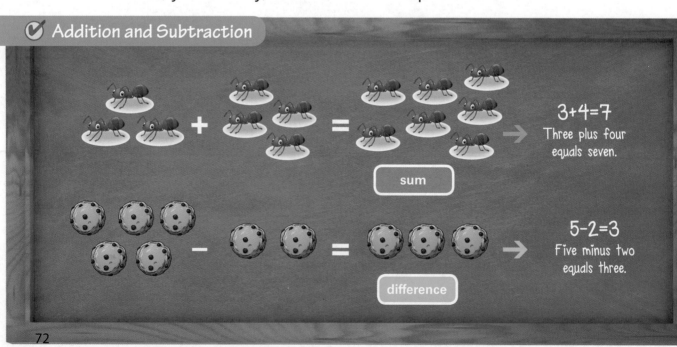

3+4=7
Three plus four
equals seven.

sum

5−2=3
Five minus two
equals three.

difference

Main Idea and Details

1 **What is the passage mainly about?**

a. The easiest way to add numbers.

b. Adding and subtracting numbers.

c. What sum and difference mean.

2 **The answer after adding two numbers together is the _____.**

a. sum   b. difference   c. subtraction

3 **What does subtract mean?**

a. Minus.   b. Take away.   c. Add.

4 **Complete the sentences.**

a. The adding together of two or more numbers is _____.

b. One plus seven _____ eight.

c. Ten _____ four equals six.

5 **Complete the outline.**

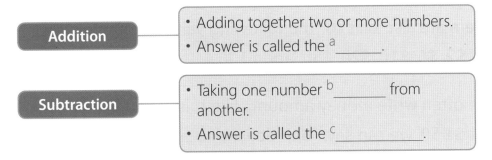

Addition
- Adding together two or more numbers.
- Answer is called the ᵃ_____.

Subtraction
- Taking one number ᵇ_____ from another.
- Answer is called the ᶜ_____.

Vocabulary Builder

Write the correct word and the meaning in Chinese.

1  ▶ taking one number away from another

_____

2  ▶ to indicate that one number is being added to another

_____

3  ▶ the sign to show you are subtracting one number from another

_____

4  ▶ the same in number and amount

_____

Counting Money

We use money to buy things.

Money can be both coins and paper bills.

All bills and coins have different values.

Key Words
- coin
- paper bill
- value
- penny
- be worth
- cent
- nickel
- dime
- quarter
- half-dollar
- amount

There are several kinds of coins and bills in American money.

A penny is worth one cent. 1 penny = 1¢

A nickel is worth five cents. 1 nickel = 5¢

A dime is worth ten cents. 1 dime = 10¢

A quarter is worth twenty-five cents. 1 quarter = 25¢

A half-dollar is worth fifty cents. 1 half-dollar = 50¢

And the value of a one-dollar coin is one hundred cents.

1 dollar = 100¢

There are also bills for the following values of money:

$1, $2, $5, $10, $20, $50, and $100.

We often write money amounts like this: $1.50.

For $1.50, we can say, "one dollar and fifty cents."

So $25.20 is "twenty-five dollars and twenty cents."

☑ American Coins

| penny | nickel | dime | quarter | half-dollar |

☑ American Bills

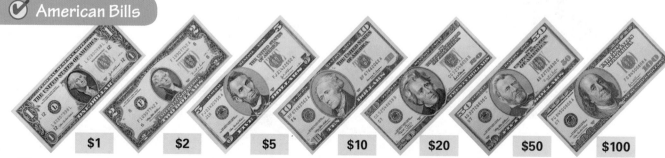

| $1 | $2 | $5 | $10 | $20 | $50 | $100 |

74

1 What is the main idea of the passage?

a. There are six different types of coins.

b. Paper money is more valuable than coins.

c. There are many types of American money.

2 How many cents are there in one dollar?

a. One. b. Twenty-five. c. One hundred.

3 What does value mean?

a. Dollar. b. Worth. c. Cent.

4 According to the passage, which statement is true?

a. A penny is worth five cents.

b. A half-dollar coin is called a quarter.

c. The biggest paper money is worth one hundred dollars.

5 Complete the outline.

American Money

Coins

- Penny = 1 cent
- Dime = 10 cents
- c _____ = 50 cents
- a _____ = 5 cents
- b _____ = 25 cents
- Dollar coin = 100 cents

Paper Bills

Comes in d _____ of $1, $2, $5, $10, $20, $50, and $100

Write the correct word and the meaning in Chinese.

 1 ▸ to have a value of
_____

 2 ▸ a coin that is worth one cent
_____

 3 ▸ a coin that is worth ten cents
_____

 4 ▸ a coin that is worth fifty cents
_____

Clocks usually have two hands: a short hand and a long hand.
The short hand shows the hour.
So, it is also called the hour hand.
The long hand shows the minute.
So, it is also called the minute hand.

How do we say the time?
It's easy. Just read the hour and then the minute.
So 2:10 is "two ten."
And 5:25 is "five twenty-five."

Sometimes, the time may be 4:30.
We can say either "four thirty" or "half past four."
Also, for 7:15, we can say "seven fifteen" or "15 minutes after seven."
And for 9:45, we can say "nine forty-five" or "15 minutes before ten."

When the long hand is on the 12 and the short hand is on the 6,
then the time is 6 o'clock. We can write it 6:00.
6:00 means the same as 6 o'clock.

Key Words

- clock
- short hand
- long hand
- hour hand
- minute hand
- either
- half
- the same as

✔ Clock

long hand
(=minute hand)

short hand
(=hour hand)

✔ Reading Time

It is **15** minutes **after 6** o'clock.

It is **15** minutes **before 7** o'clock.

Main Idea and Details

1 **What is the passage mainly about?**

a. How to tell time.

b. The hour hand.

c. The minute hand.

2 **We can write "half past five" as _____.**

a. 5:05　　　　　　　b. 5:30　　　　　　　c. 5:45

3 **What is the long hand of a clock called?**

a. The minute hand.　　　b. The second hand.　　　c. The hour hand.

4 **Answer the questions.**

a. How many hands do clocks usually have? _____

b. How do you read 4:15? _____

c. How do you read 4:45? _____

5 **Complete the outline.**

Time

Clocks

• Short hand = ᵃ_____ hand
• Long hand = ᵇ_____ hand

Reading Time

• Say the hour and the minute
• 2:10 = "two ten"
• 4:30 = "four thirty" or "ᶜ_____ past four"
• 7:15 = "seven fifteen" or "15 minutes after seven"
• 9:45 = "nine forty-five" or "15 minutes ᵈ_____ ten"
• 6:00 = "6 o'clock"

Vocabulary Builder

Write the correct word and the meaning in Chinese.

1 ▶ the short hand of a clock

_____

2 ▶ the long hand of a clock

_____

3 ▶ 30 minutes when telling the time

_____

4 ▶ equal to

_____

Reading a Calendar

We can measure time with a calendar or a clock.

A calendar shows time in days, weeks, and months.

Key Words

• measure
• calendar
• day
• week
• month
• page
• year
• row
• represent

Take a look at a calendar.

On the first page, it shows January.

January is the first month of the year.

There are 12 months in 1 year.

They are January, February, March, April, May, June, July, August, September, October, November, and December.

So your calendar has a total of twelve pages.

On each page, there are four or five rows with numbers on them.

Each number represents a day of the month.

There are 7 days in 1 week.

They are Sunday, Monday, Tuesday, Wednesday, Thursday, Friday, and Saturday.

Each row represents 1 week.

Every month has about 4 weeks.

Reading a Calendar

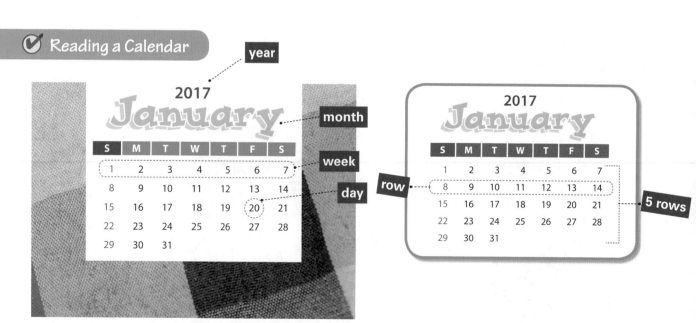

Main Idea and Details

1 **What is the passage mainly about?**

a. The days and months.

b. How to understand a calendar.

c. How many months are in a year.

2 **How many days are in one week?**

a. Four.   b. Seven.   c. Twelve.

3 **What does measure mean?**

a. Show.   b. Remember.   c. Calculate.

4 **Complete the sentences.**

a. The first month of the year is _____.

b. There are about four _____ in one month.

c. A calendar shows _____, weeks, and months.

5 **Complete the outline.**

| Calendar |
| Months | Days | Weeks |

Months
- There are a _____ months in one year.
- January, February, March, April, May, June, July, August, September, October, November, and b _____.

Days
- There are c _____ days in one week.
- Sunday, Monday, Tuesday, Wednesday, Thursday, Friday, and Saturday.

Weeks
- There are about d _____ weeks in one month.

Vocabulary Builder

Write the correct word and the meaning in Chinese.

1  ▸ a document that shows the days, weeks, and months of a year

_____

2  ▸ a period of seven days

_____

3  ▸ to stand for

_____

4  ▸ a line of things or people next to each other

_____

Vocabulary Review 7

A

Complete the sentences with the words below.

worth	adding	sum	difference
equals	coins	quarter	taking

1 Addition is _____ two or more numbers together.

2 The answer you get after you add numbers is called the _____.

3 Subtraction is _____ a number away from another one.

4 The number you have left after you subtract is called the _____.

5 You can say, "Five minus two _____ three."

6 All bills and _____ have different values.

7 A penny is _____ one cent.

8 A _____ is worth twenty-five cents.

B

Complete the sentences with the words below.

January	before	hands	hour
half	represents	days	month

1 Clocks usually have two _____: a short hand and a long hand.

2 The short hand shows the _____.

3 4:30 is "four thirty" or "_____ past four."

4 9:45 is "nine forty-five" or "15 minutes _____ ten."

5 A calendar shows time in _____, weeks, and months.

6 _____ is the first month of the year.

7 Each number _____ a day of the month.

8 Every _____ has about 4 weeks.

80

C

Write the correct word and the meaning in Chinese.

1  ▸ taking one number away from another

_____

2 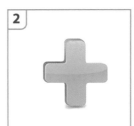 ▸ to indicate that one number is being added to another

_____

3  ▸ a coin that is worth one cent

_____

4  ▸ a coin that is worth ten cents

_____

5  ▸ the long hand of a clock

_____

6  ▸ a document that shows the days, weeks, and months of a year

_____

D

Match each word with the correct definition and write the meaning in Chinese.

1 minus (−) _____ ☐

2 equals (=) _____ ☐

3 be worth _____ ☐

4 half-dollar _____ ☐

5 hour hand _____ ☐

6 half _____ ☐

7 the same as _____ ☐

8 week _____ ☐

9 represent _____ ☐

10 row _____ ☐

a. equal to

b. to stand for

c. to have a value of

d. the short hand of a clock

e. a coin that is worth fifty cents

f. 30 minutes when telling the time

g. a period of time equal to seven days

h. a line of things or people next to each other

i. the sign to show you are subtracting one number from another

j. the sign to show the answer to a math problem

Every sentence has a subject and a verb.

Tom **runs** fast.   She **eats** pizza.

In the sentences above, *Tom* and *She* are subjects, and *runs* and *eats* are verbs.

Key Words

- sentence
- subject
- verb
- noun
- describe
- part of speech
- pronoun
- adjective
- adverb
- preposition
- location

The subject is usually a noun.
A noun names a person, place, or thing.
A verb describes the action in a sentence.
Sing, *dance*, *smile*, and *laugh* are all verbs.
Nouns and verbs are the most important parts of speech in a sentence.

We also use other parts of speech.
Pronouns are words like *I*, *he*, *she*, *it*, *we*, *you*, and *they*.
We use pronouns in place of nouns.
Adjectives are words that describe nouns and pronouns.

a **pretty** dog   a **tall** boy   a **happy** cat

Pretty, *tall*, and *happy* are all adjectives.
Adverbs describe verbs.

He cried **suddenly**.   She walks **slowly**.

Prepositions often help us with location.
They are words like *in*, *on*, *under*, *above*, and *by*.

✓ Parts of Speech

Tom runs fast.

subject   verb

She eats pizza.

pronoun   noun

a pretty dog

adjective

He cried suddenly.

adverb

The pencil is on the notebook.

preposition

Main Idea and Details

1   What is the main idea of the passage?

a. Adjectives describe nouns and pronouns.

b. There are many different parts of speech.

c. A sentence must have a subject and verb in it.

2   *I*, *he*, and *she* are examples of _____ .

a. nouns   **b.** pronouns   **c.** verbs

3   What does an adverb do?

a. It describes verbs.   **b.** It describes nouns.   **c.** It describes pronouns.

4   According to the passage, which statement is true?

a. A noun can be a person, place, or thing.

b. Pronouns are used in place of adjectives.

c. A verb describes a noun.

5   Complete the outline.

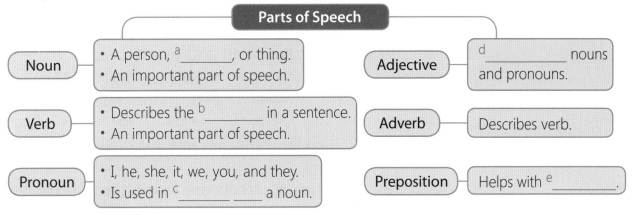

Parts of Speech

Noun
- A person, ᵃ_____, or thing.
- An important part of speech.

Verb
- Describes the ᵇ_____ in a sentence.
- An important part of speech.

Pronoun
- I, he, she, it, we, you, and they.
- Is used in ᶜ_____ ____ a noun.

Adjective
ᵈ_____ nouns and pronouns.

Adverb
Describes verb.

Preposition
Helps with ᵉ_____ .

Vocabulary Builder

Write the correct word and the meaning in Chinese.

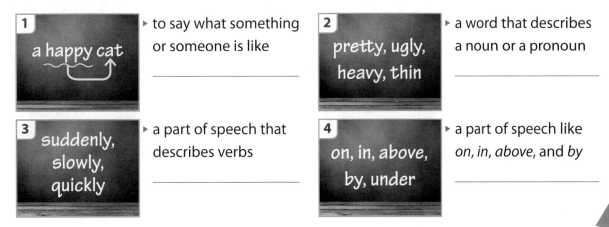

1 a happy cat ▸ to say what something or someone is like

_____

2 pretty, ugly, heavy, thin ▸ a word that describes a noun or a pronoun

_____

3 suddenly, slowly, quickly ▸ a part of speech that describes verbs

_____

4 on, in, above, by, under ▸ a part of speech like *on*, *in*, *above*, and *by*

_____

When we write, we sometimes combine two words to make one shorter word.

The shorter word is called a contraction.

We put an apostrophe(') between two words when we make a contraction.

I am = I'm	you are = you're	it is = it's
do not = don't	cannot = can't	is not = isn't

Key Words

- combine
- contraction
- apostrophe
- shorten
- abbreviate
- abbreviation
- capital
- period

Some words can be shortened or abbreviated.

Many abbreviations begin with a capital letter and end with a period.

The days of the week are often abbreviated.

Monday = Mon.	Tuesday = Tue.	Wednesday = Wed.
Thursday = Thur.	Friday = Fri.	Saturday = Sat.
Sunday = Sun.		

The months of the year are often abbreviated.

January = Jan.	February = Feb.	March = Mar.
April = Apr.	August = Aug.	September = Sept.
October = Oct.	November = Nov.	December = Dec.

The months May, June, and July are not abbreviated.

People's titles and types of streets are also often abbreviated.

Mister = Mr.	Professor = Prof.	Doctor = Dr.
Street = St.	Avenue = Ave.	Road = Rd.

✓ Contractions   **I am = I'm**   **do not = don't**   **is not = isn't**

✓ Abbreviations

Days
Mon. Tue. Wed.
Thur. Fri. Sat.
Sun.

Mr. Robertson

Dr. Smith

I live on 5th Ave.

Main Idea and Details

1 **What is the passage mainly about?**

a. How to combine or shorten words.

b. How to make an abbreviation.

c. How contractions are more common than abbreviations.

2 **Which month does not have an abbreviation?**

a. August. b. July. c. September.

3 **What does combine mean?**

a. Join. b. Shorten. c. Leave out.

4 **Answer the questions.**

a. How do you make a contraction with "I am"? _____

b. What is the abbreviation for Sunday? _____

c. What does "Dr." stand for? _____

5 **Complete the outline.**

Short Forms

Contraction
• Is a combination of two words.
• Makes one shorter word.
• Uses an ᵃ_____.

Abbreviation
• Shortens one word.
• Begins with a ᵇ_____ letter.
• Ends with a ᶜ_____.
• Can be days, months, titles, and types of streets.

Vocabulary Builder

Write the correct word and the meaning in Chinese.

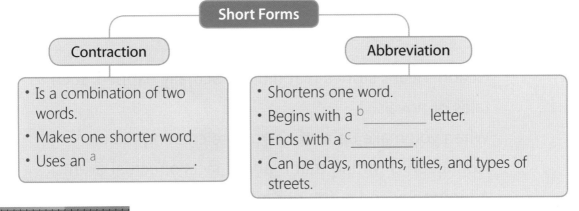

1 I'm / you're / don't / isn't ▸ a short form of a word or word group _____

2 Ave. / Dr. / Mon. / Sept. ▸ a short form of a long word _____

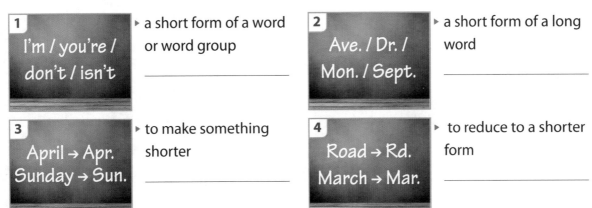

3 April → Apr. Sunday → Sun. ▸ to make something shorter _____

4 Road → Rd. March → Mar. ▸ to reduce to a shorter form _____

Types of Writing

There are many different types of writing.
Can you name some of them?

Key Words

- poem
- rhyme
- fairy tale
- magical
- fable
- novel
- fiction
- character
- biography
- autobiography
- nonfiction

A poem is a short writing that uses rhymes.

Poems often repeat regular rhymes, like *cold* and *hold*, at the ends of lines.

A fairy tale is a story for children in which magical things happen.

A short story that teaches a moral lesson is called a fable.

Animals talk and act like people in many fables.

A novel is a long story of fiction.

Novels often have many characters in them.

A biography is a true story of a person's life.

An autobiography is a biography written by the person himself.

Fiction means stories that did not actually happen, such as fairy tales or novels.

When you make up a story, you are creating fiction.

Nonfiction is writing that is about facts or actual events.

A biography and autobiography are nonfiction.

✓ Fiction

The Emperor's New Clothes

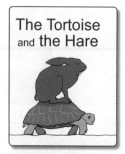

Aesop's Fables

 ✓ Nonfiction

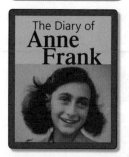

The Diary of Anne Frank

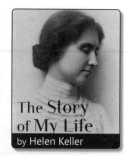

The Story of My Life

Main Idea and Details

1   **What is the passage mainly about?**

   a. The best way to write a poem.

   b. Fairy tales, fables, and novels.

   c. Types of fiction and nonfiction writing.

2   **Writing that is about facts is called _____.**

   a. a poem   **b.** nonfiction   **c.** fiction

3   **What do animals often do in fables?**

   a. They do magic.   **b.** They speak.   **c.** They make rhymes.

4   **Complete the sentences.**

   a. A long work of fiction is called a _____.

   b. A _____ is a story about a person's life.

   c. Stories that are _____ did not really happen.

5   **Complete the outline.**

   Types of Writing

   Fiction

   • Writing about stories that did not actually happen.
   • Poem = short writing using ᵃ_____
   • Fairy tale = a magical story for children
   • Fable = a short story with a moral lesson
   • ᵇ_____ = a long work of fiction

   Nonfiction

   • Writing about ᶜ_____ or actual events.
   • Biography = a story of a person's life
   • ᵈ_____ = the story of a person's life written by that person

Vocabulary Builder

Write the correct word and the meaning in Chinese.

1  ▸ a short writing that uses rhymes

_____

2  ▸ the story of a real person's life written by someone

_____

3  ▸ written stories about people and events that are not real

_____

4  ▸ writing about facts or actual events

_____

The Emperor's New Clothes

A long time ago, there lived an emperor who loved clothes. Every day, he wore the finest clothes and showed off his clothes.

Key Words

- emperor
- show off
- thief
- weave
- pretend
- loom
- terrible
- marvelous
- public
- underclothes
- admit

One day, two thieves arrived in town. They told the emperor they could make the most beautiful cloth in the world. "We are able to make magic cloth. Only smart people can see it," they said. The emperor gave them a lot of money and told them to weave the magic cloth.

Day and night, they pretended to weave cloth. But they had nothing at all on their looms. The emperor went to the room to see the cloth. But he couldn't see anything.

"This is terrible. Am I stupid?" he thought.

But out loud he said, "It looks marvelous!"

At last, the day came for the emperor to wear his new clothes in public. The emperor walked very proudly in his underclothes!

The people on the streets watched and called out,

"The clothes are beautiful."

No one would admit he could not see anything.

Then, a little child in the crowd cried out,

"He isn't wearing any clothes!"

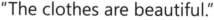

Main Idea and Details

1 **What is the passage mainly about?**

a. How two thieves tricked the emperor.

b. Making some magical cloth.

c. The emperor walking in his underclothes.

2 **According to the thieves, who could see the magic cloth?**

a. Only smart people.　　　b. Only stupid people.　　　c. All kinds of people.

3 **What does marvelous mean?**

a. Strange.　　　　　　　b. Ugly.　　　　　　　　c. Great.

4 **According to the passage, which statement is true?**

a. The people saw the emperor's magic clothes.

b. The thieves pretended to make clothes.

c. The little child was wearing magic clothes.

5 **Complete the outline.**

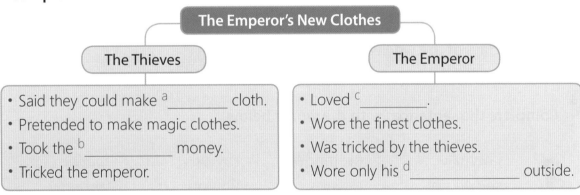

The Emperor's New Clothes

The Thieves

• Said they could make ᵃ_____ cloth.
• Pretended to make magic clothes.
• Took the ᵇ_____ money.
• Tricked the emperor.

The Emperor

• Loved ᶜ_____.
• Wore the finest clothes.
• Was tricked by the thieves.
• Wore only his ᵈ_____ outside.

Vocabulary Builder

Write the correct word and the meaning in Chinese.

 ▸ a king; the ruler of an empire

_____

 ▸ someone who steals things

_____

 ▸ to make threads into cloth

_____

 ▸ underwear; clothing you wear under your outer clothes

_____

Vocabulary > Review 8

A

Complete the sentences with the words below.

> parts of speech   subject   combine   describe
> prepositions   shortened   apostrophe   abbreviated

1   Every sentence has a _____ and a verb.

2   Nouns and verbs are the most important _____ ___ _____ in a sentence.

3   Adjectives are words that _____ nouns and pronouns.

4   _____ often help us with location.

5   When we write, we sometimes _____ two words to make one shorter word.

6   We put an _____(') between two words when we make a contraction.

7   Some words can be _____ or abbreviated.

8   The days of the week are often _____.

B

Complete the sentences with the words below.

> fairy tale   pretended   rhymes   fiction
> showed off   clothes   writing   proudly

1   There are many different types of _____.

2   Poems often repeat regular _____, like *cold* and *hold*, at the ends of lines.

3   A _____ _____ is a story for children in which magical things happen.

4   When you make up a story, you are creating _____.

5   A long time ago, there lived an emperor who loved _____.

6   Every day, the emperor wore the finest clothes and _____ _____ his clothes.

7   Day and night, the thieves _____ to weave cloth.

8   The emperor walked very _____ in his underclothes!

90

C Write the correct word and the meaning in Chinese.

1
pretty, ugly, heavy, thin

▸ a word that describes a noun or a pronoun

_____

2
suddenly, slowly, quickly

▸ a part of speech that describes verbs

_____

3
I'm / you're / don't / isn't

▸ a short form of a word or word group

_____

4
Ave. / Dr. / Mon. / Sept.

▸ a short form of a long word

_____

5
Anne Frank

▸ writing about facts or actual events

_____

6

▸ a king; the ruler of an empire

_____

D Match each word with the correct definition and write the meaning in Chinese.

1 describe _____ ☐

2 preposition _____ ☐

3 shorten _____ ☐

4 abbreviate _____ ☐

5 poem _____ ☐

6 biography _____ ☐

7 fiction _____ ☐

8 thief _____ ☐

9 weave _____ ☐

10 underclothes _____ ☐

a. to make a word shorter

b. to make threads into cloth

c. to make something shorter

d. someone who steals things

e. a short writing that uses rhymes

f. a true story of a person's life

g. a part of speech like on, in, above, and by

h. writing about stories that did not actually happen

i. to say what something is like or what happened

j. underwear; clothing you wear under your outer clothes

A World of Colors

 33

Key Words

- bright
- dark
- primary color
- mix
- combine
- secondary color

Look all around you.

You can see many different colors.

Some of them are bright. Others are dark.

All of these colors come from three primary colors.

The three primary colors are red, yellow, and blue.

With these three primary colors, we can make other colors.

How can we do that?

We simply mix two primary colors together.

We can mix red and yellow to get orange.

We can mix red and blue to get purple.

And we can combine blue and yellow to get green.

Orange, purple, and green are the three secondary colors.

In painting, primary and secondary colors are very important.

By combining different amounts of them, we can make any color in the world.

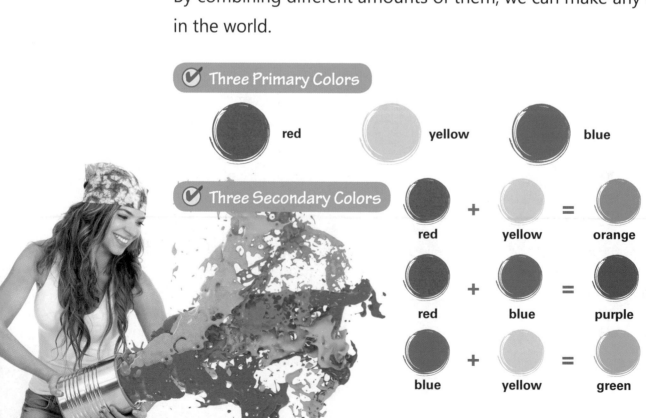

Three Primary Colors

red   yellow   blue

Three Secondary Colors

red + yellow = orange

red + blue = purple

blue + yellow = green

Main Idea and Details

1 **What is the main idea of the passage?**

    a. The primary colors make all other colors.

    b. There are three secondary colors.

    c. Colors can be bright or dark.

2 **Red, yellow, and _____ are primary colors.**

    a. orange   **b.** blue   **c.** green

3 **How can you make purple?**

    a. Mix red and yellow.

    b. Mix blue and yellow.

    c. Mix red and blue.

4 **Answer the questions.**

    a. What are the three primary colors? _____

    b. What color do you get by mixing red and yellow? _____

    c. What are orange, purple, and green? _____

5 **Complete the outline.**

Colors

Primary Colors
- Red, a_____, and blue.
- Can make all other colors with them.

Secondary Colors
- Orange, b_____, and green.
- Are made from combinations of c_____ colors.

Vocabulary Builder

Write the correct word and the meaning in Chinese.

 **1** ▸ colors that you can mix together to make any other color

_____

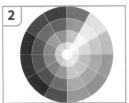 **2** ▸ colors that you can get from mixing primary colors together

_____

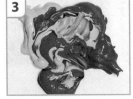 **3** ▸ to add to something else

_____

 **4** ▸ to mix (two or more things) together to form a single thing

_____

We often use lines when we draw.

Lines come in all types: straight, curved, zigzag, wavy, and spiral.

Key Words

• draw
• straight
• curved
• zigzag
• wavy
• spiral
• fine
• rough
• vertical
• horizontal
• angle
• diagonal
• shape

straight line   curved line   zigzag line
wavy line   spiral line

Lines can be fine or rough, too.

fine line   rough line

A line that goes up and down is called a vertical line.

A line that goes from left to right is called a horizontal line.

A line that moves up or down at an angle is called a diagonal line.

vertical line   horizontal line   diagonal line

Can you see the difference?

When lines join together, they make shapes.

There are three basic shapes: squares, circles, and triangles.

A square is formed by four straight lines.   □

A circle is formed by a single curved line.   ○

And a triangle is formed by three straight lines.   △

✓ **What kinds of lines can you see in the picture?**

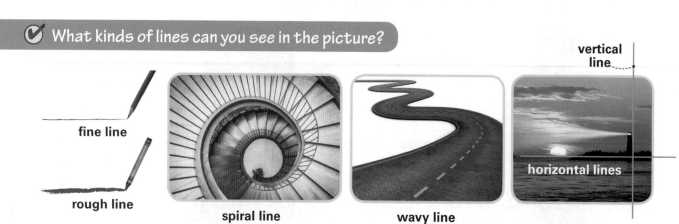

fine line

rough line

spiral line

wavy line

vertical line

horizontal lines

Main Idea and Details

1 What is the passage mainly about?

a. The most common lines.   **b.** Some lines and shapes.

c. The three basic shapes.

2 Which line goes up and down?

a. A spiral line.   b. A horizontal line.   **c.** A vertical line.

3 What does diagonal mean?

a. Straight and sloping.   **b.** Straight and curved.   **c.** Zigzag.

4 Complete the sentences.

a. _____ can be straight, curved, or wavy.

b. A horizontal line goes from left to _____.

c. A single _____ line can form a circle.

5 Complete the outline.

Lines and Shapes

Lines

- Can be straight, curved, zigzag, ᵃ_____, and spiral.
- Can be fine or rough.
- Vertical lines go up and down.
- ᵇ_____ lines go left to right.
- Diagonal lines go up or down at an angle.

Shapes

- Can be made by joining ᶜ_____ together.
- A square is formed by four straight lines.
- A circle is formed by a single curved line.
- A triangle is formed by three ᵈ_____ lines.

Vocabulary Builder

Write the correct word and the meaning in Chinese.

1 ▸ having a rounded shape
_____

2 ▸ having waves
_____

3 ▸ having a shape which winds round and round
_____

4 ▸ the shape of something
_____

35

Key Words

- instrument
- orchestra
- musician
- drummer
- violinist
- cellist
- guitarist
- pianist
- organist
- flutist
- clarinetist
- trumpeter
- trombonist

There are many kinds of instruments.

They all belong to different families.

There are percussion, string, keyboard, woodwind, and brass instruments.

In an orchestra, musicians play all of these instruments.

The drum is a percussion instrument.

A drummer plays a drum.

Violins, cellos, and guitars are three stringed instruments.

Violinists, cellists, and guitarists play them.

The piano and organ are the two most common keyboard instruments.

They are played by pianists and organists.

Flutes and clarinets are two woodwinds.

Flutists and clarinetists play these instruments.

Trumpets and trombones are two kinds of brass instruments.

A trumpeter plays the trumpet.

And a trombonist plays the trombone.

Together, all of these musicians can make beautiful music.

✔ Musicians

drummer

violinist

cellist

guitarist

organist

pianist

flutist

trumpeter

Main Idea and Details

1 **What is the passage mainly about?**

a. What an orchestra sounds like.

b. The families of musical instruments.

c. The musicians that play instruments.

2 **One woodwind instrument is the _____.**

a. cello   b. clarinet   c. trumpet

3 **What kind of instrument is a drum?**

a. A percussion instrument.   b. A keyboard instrument.

c. A brass instrument.

4 **According to the passage, which statement is true?**

a. A musician plays several kinds of instruments.

b. A flutist plays a stringed instrument.

c. Pianists and organists play keyboard instruments.

5 **Complete the outline.**

Musicians and Instruments				
Percussion	**String**	**Keyboard**	**Woodwind**	**Brass**
• Drum. • Played by a ᵃ _____.	• Violin, cello, and guitar. • Played by a ᵇ _____, cellist, and guitarist.	• Piano and organ. • Played by a pianist and organist.	• Flute and clarinet. • Played by a flutist and ᶜ _____.	• Trumpet and trombone. • Played by a trumpeter and ᵈ _____.

Vocabulary Builder

Write the correct word and the meaning in Chinese.

 **1** ▸ to be a member of an organization

_____

 **2** ▸ a person who writes, sings, or plays

_____

 **3** ▸ a musician who plays a drum

_____

 **4** ▸ a musician who plays a flute

_____

Key Words

- **composer**
- **write music**
- **compose**
- **genius**
- **tour**
- **outstanding**
- **opera**
- **symphony**
- **settle down**
- **go deaf**

Composers write, or compose, music.

Wolfgang Amadeus Mozart was one of the world's greatest composers.

He was a child genius.

He played the piano and composed music from a young age.

Mozart toured all over Europe.

He wrote many outstanding pieces of music.

He composed operas, symphonies, masses, and many other pieces.

Sadly, he died when he was only 35 years old.

Ludwig van Beethoven was another great composer.

Like Mozart, he also traveled to play music.

But he soon settled down in Vienna.

He was an excellent pianist.

But he started going deaf when he was around 30.

Still, he continued to play and compose music.

His *Ninth Symphony* is one of the world's most famous pieces of music.

Today, people still listen to Mozart's and Beethoven's music.

 Great Composers

Wolfgang Amadeus Mozart

Ludwig van Beethoven

a scene in Mozart's opera *Don Giovanni*

Main Idea and Details

1 What is the passage mainly about?

a. The life of Mozart.

b. Two outstanding composers.

c. Beethoven's *Ninth Symphony*.

2 What happened to Mozart when he was thirty-five years old?

a. He started composing music.　　b. He went deaf.　　c. He died.

3 What does toured mean?

a. Lived.　　　　　　b. Traveled.　　　　　c. Wrote.

4 Complete the sentences.

a. Mozart began to compose music when he was a _____.

b. _____ started to go deaf when he was around thirty.

c. One of Beethoven's works was the _____ _____.

5 Complete the outline.

Great Composers

Wolfgang Amadeus Mozart	Ludwig van Beethoven
• Was a child ᵃ_____. • Composed and played music as a child. • Composed ᵇ_____, symphonies, and masses. • Died when he was 35.	• Settled down in Vienna. • Began going ᶜ_____ when he was 30. • Continued to play and ᵈ_____. • His Ninth Symphony is very famous.

Vocabulary Builder

Write the correct word and the meaning in Chinese.

 **1** ▸ a person who writes music

_____

 **2** ▸ to write music

_____

 **3** ▸ a very smart or talented person

_____

 **4** ▸ to become being unable to hear

_____

A Complete the sentences with the words below.

straight	blue	secondary	rough
come in	diagonal	horizontal	mix

1   The three primary colors are red, yellow, and _____.

2   We can _____ red and yellow to get orange.

3   Orange, purple, and green are the three _____ colors.

4   Lines _____ _____ all types: straight, curved, zigzag, wavy, and spiral.

5   Lines can be fine or _____, too.

6   A line that goes from left to right is called a _____ line.

7   A line that moves up or down at an angle is called a _____ line.

8   A square is formed by four _____ lines.

B Complete the sentences with the words below.

symphonies	organists	trombonist	deaf
musicians	composers	instruments	famous

1   There are many kinds of _____.

2   In an orchestra, _____ play all of these instruments.

3   The piano and organ are played by pianists and _____.

4   A trumpeter plays the trumpet. And a _____ plays the trombone.

5   Wolfgang Amadeus Mozart was one of the world's greatest _____.

6   Mozart composed operas, _____, masses, and many other pieces.

7   Ludwig van Beethoven started going _____ when he was around 30.

8   Beethoven's *Ninth Symphony* is one of the world's most _____ pieces of music.

C

Write the correct word and the meaning in Chinese.

 ▸ colors that you can mix together to make any other color

_____

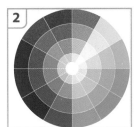 ▸ colors that you can get from mixing primary colors together

_____

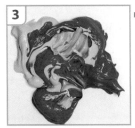 ▸ to add to something else

_____

 ▸ a shape which winds round and round

_____

 ▸ a musician who plays a drum

_____

 ▸ a person who writes music

_____

D

Match each word with the correct definition and write the meaning in Chinese.

1 combine _____ ☐

2 curved _____ ☐

3 wavy _____ ☐

4 form _____ ☐

5 belong to _____ ☐

6 musician _____ ☐

7 trumpeter _____ ☐

8 compose _____ ☐

9 genius _____ ☐

10 go deaf _____ ☐

a. having waves

b. to write music

c. to make a shape

d. rounded ; bent

e. to be a member of a group

f. to become being unable to hear

g. to join together ; to mix together

h. a musician who plays a trumpet

i. a person who plays a musical instrument very well or as job

j. someone who has very high level of intelligence or ability

Wrap-Up Test **3**

A

Write the correct word for each sentence.

> subtraction   primary   same as   weave   bills
> in place of   abbreviations   nonfiction   genius   time

1 _____ is taking a number away from another one.

2 There are several kinds of coins and _____ in American money.

3 6:00 means the _____ _____ 6 o'clock.

4 A calendar shows _____ in days, weeks, and months.

5 We use pronouns _____ _____ _____ nouns.

6 Many _____ begin with a capital letter and end with a period.

7 A biography and autobiography are _____.

8 The emperor gave them a lot of money and told them to _____ the magic cloth.

9 With the three _____ colors, we can make other colors.

10 Mozart was a child _____.

B

Write the meanings of the words in Chinese.

1 plus (+)   _____   16 describe   _____

2 minus (–)   _____   17 shorten   _____

3 equals (=)   _____   18 abbreviate   _____

4 penny   _____   19 biography   _____

5 dime   _____   20 thief   _____

6 minute hand   _____   21 primary color   _____

7 calendar   _____   22 secondary color   _____

8 be worth   _____   23 combine   _____

9 half-dollar   _____   24 curved   _____

10 row   _____   25 wavy   _____

11 adjective   _____   26 spiral   _____

12 adverb   _____   27 form   _____

13 contraction   _____   28 belong to   _____

14 fiction   _____   29 musician   _____

15 emperor   _____   30 composer   _____

● Word List
● Answers and Translations

Word List

1	**community** (n.)	社區;共同社會
2	**citizenship** (n.)	公民權;公民(或市民)身分
3	**caring** (a.)	關懷;照顧
4	**responsibility** (n.)	責任;責任感;義務
5	**honesty** (n.)	誠實
6	**courage** (n.)	膽量;勇氣
7	**fairness** (n.)	公正;公平
8	**respect** (n.)	尊敬
9	**loyalty** (n.)	忠誠;忠心
10	**look after**	照顧
11	**care for**	照料
12	**responsible** (a.)	責任
13	**honest** (a.)	誠實的
14	**truth** (n.)	實話;事實
15	**right** (a.)	正確的
16	**brave** (n.)	勇敢的
17	**treat** (v.)	對待
18	**fairly** (adv.)	公平地;公正地
19	**with respect**	尊重地
20	**loyal** (a.)	忠誠的;忠心的

02 Different Kinds of Communities

1	**urban** (a.)	城市的
2	**apartment building**	公寓大樓
3	**department store**	百貨公司
4	**rural** (a.)	農村的;田園的
5	**countryside** (n.)	鄉間;農村
6	**be surrounded by**	被……圍繞;被……包圍
7	**field** (n.)	農村的;田園的
8	**population** (n.)	人口
9	**be located**	位於;座落於
10	**far away**	遙遠的

11	**suburban** (a.)	郊區的;近郊的
12	**suburb** (n.)	近郊住宅區
13	**like** (prep.)	像;如
14	**combination** (n.)	結合;聯合
15	**as busy as**	像……那樣忙碌
16	**medium-sized** (a.)	中型的

03 The Leaders of Government

1	**leader** (n.)	領袖;領導者
2	**mayor** (n.)	市長;鎮長
3	**vote for**	投票
4	**governor** (n.)	(美國各州的)州長;地方長官
5	**lead** (v.)	領導;帶領;指揮 * 動詞三態 lead-led-led
6	**elect** (v.)	選舉
7	**run** (v.)	管理;指揮
8	**provide for**	提供
9	**needs** (n.)	需要;需求
10	**education** (n.)	教育
11	**safety** (n.)	安全;平安
12	**transportation** (n.)	大眾運輸工具
13	**make sure**	確保
14	**law** (n.)	法律
15	**protect** (v.)	保護;防護
16	**prevent...from...**	阻止;制止
17	**harm** (v.)	損傷;傷害
18	**in harmony**	和睦;融洽

04 Martin Luther King, Jr.

1	**grow up**	成長 * 動詞三態 grow-grew-grown
2	**in the middle of**	在……當中
3	**poorly** (adv.)	貧窮地;貧乏地
4	**right** (n.)	權利
5	**dream** (v.)	夢想;理想
6	**in peace**	和平
7	**march** (n.)	遊行抗議;遊行示威

8	give a speech	演說；演講
9	arrest (v.)	逮捕；拘留
10	give up	放棄；讓出
11	nonviolence (n.)	非暴力
12	win (v.)	贏得；獲得
		* 動詞三態
		win-won-won
13	Nobel Peace Prize	諾貝爾和平獎
14	pass (v.)	通過
15	Civil Rights Act	（美國）公民權法案
16	unfair (a.)	不公平的；不公正的
17	African-American (n.)	非裔美國人
18	guarantee (v.)	保證
19	honor (v.)	尊敬；敬重
20	celebrate (v.)	慶祝

05 Many Jobs

1	job (n.)	職業；工作
2	earn money	賺錢；掙錢
3	get paid	支薪；領薪水
4	hourly (adv.)	每小時一次地
5	weekly (adv.)	每週；一週一次地
6	monthly (adv.)	每月一次；每月
7	goods (n.)	商品；貨物
8	produce (v.)	製造；生產
9	factory (n.)	工廠
10	product (n.)	產物；產品
11	service (n.)	服務
12	professional (a.)	專門職業的
13	require (v.)	需要
14	engineer (n.)	工程師；技術員

06 Volunteers and Community Jobs

1	for free	免費
2	volunteer (n.)	志願者；義工
3	hospital (n.)	醫院
4	assist...in...	協助……做……
5	take care of	照顧

6	patient (n.)	病患；病人
7	homeless (a.)	無家可歸的
8	homeless shelter	遊民收容所
9	food bank	食物銀行
10	unfortunate (a.)	運氣不好的；不幸的
11	be in trouble	陷入了麻煩
12	earthquake (n.)	地震
13	flood (n.)	洪水；水災
14	special (a.)	專門的
15	whole (a.)	全部；全體
16	firefighter (n.)	消防員
17	police officer	警察
18	improve (v.)	改善；改進

07 What Is a Map?

1	map (n.)	地圖
2	drawing (n.)	繪畫；描畫
3	look like	看起來像……；外觀相似
4	view (n.)	視域；視野
5	neighborhood (n.)	鄰近地區
6	entire (a.)	全部的
7	helpful (a.)	有用的；有益的
8	location (n.)	位置；場所；所在地
9	symbol (n.)	符號；記號
10	stand for	代表……
11	real (a.)	真實的；真正的
12	map key	地圖索引
13	title (n.)	標題；題目
14	feature (n.)	特徵；特色

08 Maps and Directions

1	a few	幾個；有一些
2	find (v.)	發現；找出
3	compass rose	羅盤玫瑰
4	main (a.)	主要的；最重要的
5	direction (n.)	方向；方位
6	point out	指出

7	straight up	正上方
8	be marked with	用……做記號
9	straight down	正下方
10	scale (n.)	地圖比例尺；地圖縮尺
11	calculate (v.)	計算；估算
12	distance (n.)	距離
13	represent (v.)	表示；象徵；意味著
14	away (adv.)	遠離

09 Natural Resources

1	natural (a.)	自然的；天然的
2	resource (n.)	資源
3	natural resources	天然資源；自然資源
4	useful (a.)	有用的；有幫助的
5	nature (n.)	自然；自然界
6	be full of	充滿……的
7	be ready	現成的；現有的；立即可得到的
8	energy (n.)	能源；能量（指熱、電等）
9	breathe (v.)	呼吸；吸入
10	coal (n.)	煤
11	drive (v.)	駕駛
12	electricity (n.)	電；電流；電力
13	cotton (n.)	棉花
14	wool (n.)	羊毛

10 Caring for Our Resources

1	careful (a.)	仔細的；小心的
2	use up	用完；耗盡
3	save (v.)	節省
4	in the future	將來
5	conserve (v.)	保存；保護；節省
6	reuse (v.)	再用；重新使用；重複利用
7	as much as	像……那樣多
8	use less	減少使用
9	reduce (v.)	減少；降低
10	the amount of …	……的總量
11	turn off	關掉

12	brush one's teeth	刷牙
13	recycle (v.)	回收；再利用
14	collect (v.)	集中；收集
15	item (n.)	項目；品目
16	put…into…	將……放入……
17	recycling bin	資源回收筒
18	again and again	一再地

11 Native Americans

1	Native American	美國原住民
2	ancestor (n.)	祖宗；祖先
3	pass (v.)	相傳
4	form (v.)	組織；成立
5	one's own	某人的
6	tribe (n.)	部落；種族
7	language (n.)	語言
8	custom (n.)	習慣；風俗；習俗
9	grow (v.)	生長；成長；發育
		* 動詞三態 grow-grew-grown
10	the Lakota	美國拉科塔族
11	tepee (n.)	（美國印第安人的）圓錐形帳篷
12	the Pueblo	美國普韋布洛族
13	adobe (n.)	曬乾的泥磚
14	the Iroquois	美國依洛郭亦族
15	longhouse (n.)	長形房屋
16	pottery (n.)	陶器
17	craftwork (n.)	手工藝品
18	carry on	繼續；進行

12 Early American Empires

1	the Americas	美洲（涵蓋北美、中美和南美34個國家）
2	establish (v.)	建立；設立
3	empire (n.)	帝國
4	the Mayans	瑪雅族
5	temple (n.)	神殿；聖堂
6	palace (n.)	皇宮；宮殿

7	civilization (n.)	文明;文明國家
8	advanced (a.)	先進的
9	ancient (a.)	古代的;古老的
10	worship (v.)	崇拜;敬仰;敬神
11	nature god	自然神
12	the Aztecs	阿茲提克人
13	modern-day (a.)	現代的;當代的;今日的
14	warlike (a.)	好戰的;尚武的;英勇的
15	devote (v.)	獻給;將……奉獻給
16	incredible (a.)	不可思議的;驚人的

13 What Are Living Things?

1	either (conj.)	或;任一的
2	living (a.)	有生命的;活著的
3	nonliving (a.)	無生命的;非活體的
4	nonliving thing	非生物
5	living thing	生物;動物
6	shelter (n.)	遮蓋物;躲避處;避難所
7	safe (a.)	安全的;無危險的
8	protect (v.)	保護;防護
9	environment (n.)	環境;四周狀況
10	room (n.)	空間;場所
11	move around	到處移動
12	space (n.)	空間

14 How Do Living Things Survive in the Cold?

1	Antarctica (n.)	南極洲
2	temperature (n.)	溫度;氣溫
3	below freezing	低於零度;低於冰點
4	still (adv.)	還;仍舊
5	manage to	達成;設法
6	survive (v.)	活下來;倖存
7	adapt (n.)	使適應;使適合
8	layer (n.)	層
9	fat (n.)	脂肪
10	stay warm	保持暖和
11	feather (n.)	羽毛

12	Arctic (a.)	北極的
13	tundra (n.)	苔原;凍土地帶;凍原
14	fur (n.)	毛皮
15	human (n.)	人類
16	clothing (n.)	衣服;衣著

15 How Do Plants Grow and Change?

1	life cycle	生命週期
2	seed (n.)	種子;籽
3	nutrient (n.)	營養物;滋養物
4	soil (n.)	土;泥土;土壤
5	germinate (v.)	發芽;生長
6	sprout (v.)	芽;新芽;嫩芽
7	grow into	成長為;漸成;變為
8	bean plant	碗豆
9	closely (adv.)	緊密地;仔細地
10	plant (n.)	植物;苗
11	water (v.)	灌溉
12	grow down	變短;縮小;減少
13	seedling (n.)	幼苗;秧苗
14	fertilize (v.)	使肥沃;施肥於

16 How Do Plants Survive in the Desert?

1	everywhere (adv.)	到處;無論何處
2	even (adv.)	甚至
3	desert (n.)	沙漠;荒野
4	harsh (a.)	嚴酷的;惡劣的
5	little (a.)	少;不多的
6	few (a.)	很少數的;幾乎沒有的
7	cactus (n.)	仙人掌
8	spiny (a.)	多刺的;尖刺狀的
9	store (v.)	儲存;儲藏
10	without (prep.)	無;沒有;不
11	spread out	攤開;散開
12	capture (v.)	捕捉;奪取

17 Kinds of Animals

1	**in common**	共同的;共有的
2	**mammal** (n.)	哺乳動物
3	**give birth to**	生(孩子)
4	**young** (n.)	幼小動物;幼禽總稱
5	**feed** (v.)	哺乳;餵
6	**bird** (n.)	鳥
7	**beak** (n.)	鳥嘴;喙
8	**lay eggs**	產卵;生蛋
9	**hatch** (v.)	孵出
10	**reptile** (n.)	爬行動物;爬蟲類
11	**covered with**	被……覆蓋
12	**scale** (n.)	鱗;殼
13	**alligator** (n.)	鱷魚
14	**amphibian** (n.)	兩棲動物
15	**salamander** (n.)	蠑螈
16	**fin** (n.)	鰭
17	**angelfish** (n.)	扁鮫;神仙魚
18	**shark** (n.)	鯊魚

18 Insects

1	**millions of**	百萬的;許許多多的
2	**species** (n.)	物種;種類
3	**insect** (n.)	昆蟲
4	**butterfly** (n.)	蝴蝶
5	**cricket** (n.)	蟋蟀
6	**similarity** (n.)	類似;相似
7	**body part**	身體的部分
8	**thorax** (n.)	(昆蟲的)胸部
9	**abdomen** (n.)	腹;下腹;腹部
10	**antennae** (n.)	(動物的)觸角;觸鬚
11	**pair** (n.)	一雙;一對;一副
12	**though** (conj.)	可是;然而;不過
13	**female** (a.)	女性的;雌性的
14	**stinger** (n.)	(昆蟲的)螫針;刺

19 The Life Cycle of an Animal

1	**life cycle**	生命週期
2	**stage** (n.)	階段;舞台
3	**go through**	經歷
4	**birth** (n.)	分娩;出生
5	**growth** (n.)	生長;成長;發育
6	**reproduction** (n.)	生殖;繁育
7	**death** (n.)	死;死亡
8	**helpless** (a.)	無力照顧自己的;無助的
9	**take care of**	照顧
10	**grow up**	成長
11	**look like**	看起來像……
12	**parents** (n.)	雙親
13	**take** (v.)	需要;花費
14	**adult** (n.)	成年人
15	**mature** (a.)	成熟的
16	**reproduce** (v.)	生殖;繁育
17	**finally** (adv.)	最後;終於
18	**reach** (v.)	到達;達到

20 The Life Cycle of a Frog

1	**frog** (n.)	青蛙
2	**in fact**	事實上
3	**unique** (a.)	唯一的;獨一無二的
4	**tadpole** (n.)	蝌蚪
5	**resemble** (v.)	像;類似
6	**not…at all**	一點也不……
7	**tail** (n.)	尾巴;尾部
8	**gills** (n.)	(魚)鰓
9	**breathe** (v.)	呼吸;呼氣;吸氣
10	**grow older**	變得更年長
11	**get ready to**	準備好
12	**on land**	在陸地上
13	**develop** (v.)	發展;發育
14	**become** (v.)	變成;成為;變得

* 動詞三態
become-became-become

15	lungs (n.)	肺
16	onto (prep.)	到⋯⋯上
17	most of	大多數
18	life (n.)	生活；生命；人生

21 What Are Food Chains?

1	food chain	食物鏈
2	order (n.)	順序；次序
3	at the bottom of	在⋯⋯底部
4	link (n.)	（鏈狀物的）環；節
5	plant eater	草食性動物
6	grasshopper (n.)	蚱蜢
7	squirrel (n.)	松鼠
8	meat eater	食肉性動物
9	hawk (n.)	鷹
10	hunt (v.)	追獵
11	be hunted by	被⋯⋯追捕
12	at the top of	在⋯⋯頂端

22 The Ocean Food Chain

1	exist (v.)	存在
2	ocean (n.)	海洋；海
3	life form	生命形式
4	get eaten by	被⋯⋯吃
5	creature (n.)	生物；動物
6	algae (n.)	水藻；海藻
7	plankton (n.)	浮游生物
8	consume (v.)	消耗；花費；耗盡
9	slightly (adv.)	輕微地；稍微地
10	shellfish (n.)	貝；有殼的水生動物
11	clam (n.)	蛤蜊
12	shrimp (n.)	蝦
13	crab (n.)	蟹
14	cod (n.)	鱈魚
15	mackerel (n.)	鯖
16	flatfish (n.)	比目魚
17	tuna (n.)	鮪魚

18	swordfish (n.)	劍魚
19	killer whale	虎鯨；殺人鯨
20	great white shark	大白鯊

23 What Is the Solar System?

1	solar system	太陽系
2	be made up of	由⋯⋯構成；由⋯⋯組成
3	planet (n.)	行星
4	object (n.)	物體；物件
5	move around	繞著⋯⋯轉
6	orbit (n.)	（天體等的）運行軌道
7	in order of	依⋯⋯順序
8	Mercury (n.)	水星
9	Venus (n.)	金星
10	Earth (n.)	地球
11	Mars (n.)	火星
12	Jupiter (n.)	木星
13	Saturn (n.)	土星
14	Uranus (n.)	天王星
15	Neptune (n.)	海王星
16	path (n.)	路線；軌道
17	be called	被稱為⋯⋯
18	distance (n.)	距離；路程

24 What Causes the Seasons?

1	season (n.)	季節
2	throughout (prep.)	遍及；遍布
3	cause (v.)	導致；使發生；引起
4	while (conj.)	當⋯⋯的時候
5	rotate (v.)	旋轉；轉動
6	complete (v.)	完成；結束
7	tilt (v.)	傾斜；偏斜
8	be tilted	傾斜的；偏斜的
9	direction (n.)	方向；方位
10	toward (prep.)	向；朝
11	sun's rays	太陽光
12	directly (adv.)	直接地；筆直地
13	away from	遠離；從某地離開
14	repeat (v.)	重複；重做

25　Addition and Subtraction

1	**addition** (n.)	加法
2	**add** (v.)	將……相加
3	**suppose** (n.)	假定
4	**join** (v.)	參加
5	**sum** (n.)	總和
6	**plus (+)** (v.)	加；加上
7	**equals (=)** (v.)	等於
8	**subtraction** (n.)	減；減算
9	**take away**	帶走；拿走
10	**take** (v.)	拿；取
11	**be left**	剩下
12	**subtract** (v.)	減；減去
13	**difference** (n.)	差額
14	**minus (-)** (v.)	減；減去

26　Counting Money

1	**coin** (n.)	硬幣；錢幣
2	**(paper) bill** (n.)	（紙）鈔票
3	**value** (n.)	價值；價格
4	**several** (a.)	幾個的；數個的
5	**penny** (n.)	一分；一分硬幣
6	**be worth**	有……的價值；值……
7	**cent** (n.)	一分值的硬幣
8	**nickel** (n.)	五分錢
9	**dime** (n.)	十分錢
10	**quarter** (n.)	25分錢
11	**half-dollar** (n.)	半毛錢
12	**following** (a.)	下面的；下述的

27　Telling Time

1	**clock** (n.)	時鐘
2	**short hand**	短針
3	**long hand**	長針
4	**hour** (n.)	小時
5	**hour hand**	時針
6	**minute** (n.)	分鐘
7	**minute hand**	分針
8	**half** (n.)	半；一半；二分之一
9	**o'clock** (adv.)	……點鐘
10	**the same as**	與……相同

28　Reading a Calendar

1	**measure** (v.)	量；測量
2	**calendar** (n.)	日曆
3	**day** (n.)	一天（24小時）；日
4	**week** (n.)	週；一星期
5	**month** (n.)	月
6	**take a look at**	看一看
7	**January** (n.)	一月
8	**February** (n.)	二月
9	**March** (n.)	三月
10	**April** (n.)	四月
11	**May** (n.)	五月
12	**June** (n.)	六月
13	**July** (n.)	七月
14	**August** (n.)	八月
15	**September** (n.)	九月
16	**October** (n.)	十月
17	**November** (n.)	十一月
18	**December** (n.)	十二月
19	**row** (n.)	列；排
20	**represent** (v.)	代表

29 Parts of Speech

1	**sentence** (n.)	句子
2	**subject** (n.)	主題；題目
3	**verb** (n.)	動詞
4	**noun** (n.)	名詞
5	**name** (n.)	名字；姓名；名稱
6	**describe** (v.)	描寫；描繪；敘述
7	**action** (n.)	行動；行為
8	**part of speech**	詞類
9	**pronoun** (n.)	代名詞
10	**in place of**	代替
11	**adjective** (n.)	形容詞
12	**adverb** (n.)	副詞
13	**suddenly** (adv.)	突然地；忽然地
14	**preposition** (n.)	介係詞

30 Contractions and Abbreviations

1	**combine** (v.)	結合；聯合
2	**contraction** (n.)	縮短；縮約；縮短形；縮約形式
3	**apostrophe** (n.)	撇號（'）；省略符號；所有格符號
4	**shorten** (v.)	使變短；縮短
5	**abbreviate** (v.)	縮寫；省略
6	**abbreviation** (n.)	縮寫字；縮寫式
7	**capital letter**	大寫字母
8	**period** (n.)	句號
9	**title** (n.)	標題；題目
10	**type** (n.)	類型；型式
11	**professor** (n.)	教授
12	**street** (n.)	街；街道
13	**avenue** (n.)	大街；大道
14	**road** (n.)	公路；路

31 Types of Writing

1	**poem** (n.)	詩
2	**rhyme** (n.)	韻；韻腳；押韻
3	**regular** (a.)	有規則的；有規律的
4	**fairy tale**	童話
5	**magical** (a.)	有魔力的；神祕的
6	**moral** (a.)	（寓言等的）寓意
7	**lesson** (n.)	教訓；課程
8	**fable** (n.)	寓言
9	**novel** (n.)	（長篇）小說
10	**fiction** (n.)	（總稱）小說
11	**biography** (n.)	傳記
12	**autobiography** (n.)	自傳
13	**make up**	虛構；編造
14	**nonfiction** (n.)	非小說類的寫實文學作品
15	**fact** (n.)	事實
16	**actual event**	真實事件

32 The Emperor's New Clothes

1	**emperor** (n.)	皇帝；國王
2	**clothes** (n.)	衣著；衣服
3	**wear** (v.)	穿著 * 動詞三態 　wear-wore-worn
4	**fine** (a.)	漂亮的；好看的 * 原級：fine 　比較級：finer 　最高級：finest
5	**show off**	炫耀
6	**thief** (n.)	賊；小偷
7	**be able to**	能夠
8	**magic** (n.)	魔法的；有魔力的
9	**cloth** (n.)	布匹；織物；衣料
10	**weave** (v.)	織；編
11	**pretend to**	假裝；裝作
12	**loom** (n.)	織布機
13	**terrible** (a.)	可怕的；駭人的

14	**marvelous** (a.)	令人驚歎的；非凡的；不可思議的
15	**underclothes** (n.)	內衣；襯衣
16	**call out**	大聲喊出
17	**admit** (v.)	承認；准許
18	**crowd** (n.)	人群

33 A World of Colors

1	**look around**	環顧
2	**primary** (a.)	基本的；主要的
3	**primary color**	原色
4	**mix** (v.)	混合；混入
5	**purple** (n.)	紫色
6	**combine** (v.)	結合；聯合
7	**secondary** (a.)	第二的；第二位的
8	**secondary color**	第二次色
9	**painting** (n.)	繪畫
10	**amount** (n.)	數量

34 Lines and Shapes

1	**line** (n.)	線條
2	**draw** (v.)	畫；繪製
3	**straight** (a.)	平直的；平的
4	**curved** (a.)	彎曲的
5	**zigzag** (a.)	曲折的
6	**wavy** (a.)	波浪形的
7	**spiral** (a.)	螺旋形的
8	**fine** (a.)	纖細的；尖細的
9	**rough** (a.)	粗糙的；表面不平的
10	**vertical** (a.)	垂直的；豎的
11	**horizontal** (a.)	水平的；橫的
12	**diagonal** (a.)	對角線的
13	**form** (v.)	形成；構成
14	**be formed by**	由……形成；由……構成

35 Musicians and Their Instruments

1	**instrument** (n.)	樂器
2	**belong to**	屬於
3	**percussion** (n.)	打擊（樂器）
4	**string** (n.)	弦（樂器）
5	**keyboard** (n.)	鍵盤（樂器）
6	**woodwind** (n.)	木管（樂器）
7	**brass** (n.)	銅管（樂器）
8	**musician** (n.)	音樂家
9	**drummer** (n.)	鼓手
10	**stringed** (a.)	有弦的；弦樂器的
11	**violinist** (n.)	小提琴手
12	**cellist** (n.)	大提琴手
13	**guitarist** (n.)	吉他手
14	**common** (a.)	普遍的；常見的
15	**pianist** (n.)	鋼琴家；鋼琴演奏者
16	**organist** (n.)	風琴手；風琴演奏家
17	**flutist** (n.)	長笛手；吹長笛者
18	**clarinetist** (n.)	黑管手；豎笛手
19	**trumpeter** (n.)	小號手；小號吹奏者
20	**trombonist** (n.)	長號手

36 Mozart and Beethoven

1	**composer** (n.)	作曲家
2	**write music**	作曲
3	**compose** (v.)	創作（詩歌、樂曲）；為……譜曲
4	**great** (a.)	偉大的；傑出的 *原級：great 　比較級：greater 　最高級：greatest
5	**genius** (n.)	天才
6	**tour** (v.)	旅行；巡迴演出
7	**outstanding** (a.)	傑出的；優秀的
8	**symphony** (n.)	交響曲；交響樂
9	**mass** (n.)	彌撒曲
10	**settle down**	定居下來
11	**excellent** (a.)	優秀的；一流的；卓越的
12	**go deaf**	變聾

Answers and Translations

01 Building Citizenship 建立公民品格

我們共同生活在一個社會中。
如何才能成為一個更好的社會公民呢？
有七種方式能夠展現好公民特質：關懷他人、有責任感、誠實、有勇氣、待人公平、尊重他人、處世忠誠。

關懷他人代表思慮他人的需要，
好公民會照顧鄰居並照料他人。
有責任感就是做好份內之事，
努力去當一個盡責的人。

好公民要誠實。
誠實意味著說實話。
做正確的事並不容易，
所以好公民也需要勇氣。
有勇氣的意思是即便遇到困難也會勇敢面對。
好公民待人公平，並且尊重他人。
另外，好公民處世忠誠，無論是對朋友、家庭、社會或是國家，都是如此。

• **Main Idea and Details**

1 **(c)**　　2 **(a)**　　3 **(a)**
4 a. **community**　　b. **brave**　　c. **treat**
5 a. **Look**　　b. **truth**　　c. **fair**　　d. **loyal**

• **Vocabulary Builder**

1 **citizenship** 公民品格；公民權；公民（或市民）身分
2 **fairness** 公正；公平
3 **courage** 勇氣　　4 **loyalty** 忠誠；忠心

02 Different Kinds of Communities 形形色色的社會區域

社會區域的樣貌有很多型式，
有些是小型區域，有些是大型區域。

都市型區域位於都市，
許多人在都市裡生活和工作。
都市的人們通常住在公寓大廈裡。
超級市場、百貨公司和其他商店都他們的住宅附近。

農村型區域位於鄉間，
通常，鄉間區域被土地和田野環繞，
鄉間居民人口稀少，大多住在獨棟房舍中。
商店和大樓通常離家很遠。

郊區區域靠近都市，
是鄰近大城市的小市區。
它們像都市和鄉村的綜合體。
大多數郊區不像都市那麼繁忙，
擁有中型人口數量。

• **Main Idea and Details**

1 **(b)**　　2 **(c)**　　3 **(b)**　　4 **(c)**
5 a. **city**　　b. **countryside**　　c. **urban**　　d. **population**

• **Vocabulary Builder**

1 **urban** 城市的　　2 **population** 人口
3 **be surrounded by** 被……圍繞；被……包圍
4 **rural** 農村的；田園的

03 The Leaders of Government 政府的領導者

在美國，各式區域和州都有一位領導者，
民眾能夠選擇他們的領導者。

在社區裡，市長是領導者。
社區的市民透過投票選出領導者；
在州裡，州長是領導者。
每州的公民透過投票選出州長；
總統領導整個國家。
每四年，全體公民會投票選出總統來管理國家。

領導者提供社區、州和國家內的人民需求。
這些需求包括了教育、安全和交通運輸。
每位領導者也會確保人民遵守法律。
法律非常重要，
法律保護人民，也防止他們傷害他人。
法律幫助人民和睦相處。

• **Main Idea and Details**

1 **(b)**　　2 **(c)**　　3 **(b)**
4 a. **the president**　　b. **citizens; people**
　 c. **education, safety, and transportation**
5 a. **State**　　b. **needs**　　c. **law**

• **Vocabulary Builder**

1 **mayor** 市長　　2 **needs** 需要；需求
3 **safety** 安全　　4 **transportation** 交通運輸

04 Martin Luther King, Jr. 馬丁・路德・金恩

馬丁・路德・金恩是一位偉大的領袖，
他在1900年代中期成長於美國南方。
馬丁・路德・金恩是一位黑人，
在當時，許多美國人並不善待黑人。

金恩博士堅信所有人都該被平等對待，
他的夢想是讓所有人種都能和平共處。
金恩博士率眾遊行並發表演說，
雖然多次遭到逮捕，但他從不放棄。
他深信非暴力改革的理念。

1964年時，他獲頒諾貝爾和平獎。
同年度，美國政府也通過民權法案。
此法案改變了對非裔美國人不平等的律法，
保障所有美國人享有同樣的權利。

為了紀念馬丁・路德・金恩，
人們每年都會在一月慶祝馬丁・路德・金恩紀念日。

• Main Idea and Details
1 **(a)**　　2 **(a)**　　3 **(c)**
4 a. **South**　　b. **arrested**　　c. **Civil Rights**
5 a. **treated**　　b. **speeches**　　c. **January**
• Vocabulary Builder
1 **arrest** 逮捕；拘留　　2 **give up** 放棄；讓出
3 **nonviolence** 非暴力
4 **Civil Rights Act** （美國）公民權法案

Vocabulary Review 1

A　1 **fairly**　　　　　2 **Responsibility**
　　3 **Honesty**　　　　4 **loyal**
　　5 **city**　　　　　　6 **countryside**
　　7 **located**　　　　8 **suburban**

B　1 **vote**　　　　　　2 **governor**
　　3 **elect**　　　　　　4 **prevent**
　　5 **poorly**　　　　　6 **right**
　　7 **unfair**　　　　　8 **guaranteed**

C　1 **courage** 膽量；勇氣　　2 **urban** 城市的
　　3 **rural** 農村的；田園的　　4 **mayor** 市長；鎮長
　　5 **transportation** 運輸；輸送　　6 **arrest** 逮捕；拘留

D　1 公民權；公民（或市民）　　2 公正；公平 **d**
　　　身分 **h**
　　3 忠誠；忠心 **i**　　　4 人口 **f**
　　5 被⋯⋯圍繞；被⋯⋯包圍 **b**　6 需要；需求 **a**
　　7 安全；平安 **c**　　8 放棄；讓出 **e**
　　9 非暴力 **j**　　10 （美國）公民權法案 **g**

05 Many Jobs 各行各業

許多人都有工作。
工作就是人們所做的勞務。
多數人為了賺錢而工作。
他們通常領時薪、週薪或月薪。
有了薪水，他們就能照顧自己和家人。

工作有很多種，
有些勞工利用種植或製造商品來賺錢。
農夫栽種我們每日所吃的糧食；
工廠工人製造許多我們的日用品。

有些勞工靠服務他人賺錢，
例如服務生、廚師、快遞人員和業務員。
這些職業的工作者提供服務給他人。

有些人則從事專業的工作，
專業工作者需要接受專門的教育和訓練，
像是醫生、律師、工程師和藝術家。

• Main Idea and Details
1 **(a)**　　2 **(c)**　　3 **(b)**　　4 **(b)**
5 a. **products**　　b. **services**　　c. **lawyer**
• Vocabulary Builder
1 **job** 工作；職業　　2 **earn money** 賺錢；掙錢
3 **goods** 商品；貨物　　4 **service** 服務

06 Volunteers and Community Jobs 志工與社區工作

有些人並沒有從他們的工作賺得薪水，
他們無償付出並幫助他人，
我們稱這些人為「志工」。

志工擔任許多重要的工作。
有些人在醫院擔任志工，
他們協助醫生和護士照護病患。
有些人在遊民收容所或食物銀行當志工。
他們幫忙照顧更加不幸的人。
當民眾因地震或洪水而身陷困境時，志工會伸出援手。

還有許多能幫助整個社群的特別行業。
像是消防員和警察。
他們為整個社群工作，而社群也給予配薪。

所有這些志工和社群工作都是為了增進社群福祉。
他們使我們的社區更加美好。

• Main Idea and Details
1 **(c)**　　2 **(a)**　　3 **(a)**
4 a. **They earn no money.**
　 b. **hospitals, homeless shelters, and food banks**
　 c. **firefighter and police officer**
5 a. **food banks**　b. **floods**　c. **Firefighters**　d. **community**
• Vocabulary Builder
1 **volunteer** 志願者；義工　　2 **homeless shelter** 遊民收容所
3 **earthquake** 地震　　4 **flood** 洪水；水災

07 What Is a Map? 地圖是什麼？

地圖是一個區域的描繪圖，
它看起來像是一幅鳥瞰圖。
地圖可以呈現城市、州或國家，
它也可以呈現一塊小區域或全世界。

地圖非常實用，
我們大多用它來找尋位置，
我們也會用地圖來表示兩地之間的距離。

大部分的地圖上會有符號。
符號就是地圖上代表實際地物的圖片。
符號可以代表房屋、大樓、河流、山嶺、街道等。
地圖有地圖索引，
地圖索引說明地圖上符號的代表意義。
地圖也有標題，
標題告訴你這份地圖的顯示區域。
這些地圖特徵幫助我們閱讀和使用地圖。

- **Main Idea and Details**

1 (b)　　2 (b)　　3 (a)

4 a. **above**　　b. **locations**　　c. **Map features**

5 a. **views**　　b. **pictures**　　c. **symbols**

- **Vocabulary Builder**

1 **map** 地圖　　　　　　2 **location** 位置；場所；所在地

3 **map key** 地圖索引　　4 **stand for** 代表……

---

08 Maps and Directions 地圖與方位

當我們使用地圖之前，必須先學會一些事項。
首先，我們必須找到羅盤玫瑰。
羅盤玫瑰告訴我們地圖上的四個主要方位。
它會標示出北、南、東、西的方向。
在大多數的地圖上，北方在地圖的正上方，以「N」標示。
東方在右邊；南方在正下方；西方在左邊。

地圖也有比例尺。
所有地圖都比所代表的實際地點還小。
比例尺能讓我們推估兩地的實際距離。
舉例來說，地圖比例尺若用一公分代表十公里，
在這張地圖上，兩個城市如果相距三公分，
實際上，兩個城市則相距三十公里。

- **Main Idea and Details**

1 (b)　　2 (a)　　3 (c)　　4 (c)

5 a. **down**　　b. **left**　　c. **distance**　　d. **smaller**

- **Vocabulary Builder**

1 **compass rose** 羅盤玫瑰　　2 **direction** 方向；方位

3 **map scale** 地圖比例尺；地圖縮尺

4 **represent** 表示；象徵；意味著

Vocabulary Review 2

A　1 **earn**　　　　　　2 **get paid**

　　3 **growing**　　　　4 **Professional**

　　5 **free**　　　　　　6 **food banks**

　　7 **community**　　　8 **police officer**

B　1 **drawing**　　　　2 **locations**

　　3 **symbols**　　　　4 **features**

　　5 **directions**　　　6 **marked**

　　7 **real area**　　　8 **distance**

C　1 **goods** 商品；貨物　　2 **volunteer** 志願者；義工

　　3 **flood** 洪水；水災　　4 **map key** 地圖索引

　　5 **compass rose** 羅盤玫瑰　6 **stand for** 代表……

D　1 工作；職業 **b**　　　2 賺錢；掙錢 **d**

　　3 服務 **f**　　　　　　4 遊民收容所 **i**

　　5 地震 **h**　　　　　　6 地圖 **g**

　　7 位置；場所；所在地 **c**　8 方向；方位 **e**

　　9 地圖比例尺；地圖縮尺 **j**

　　10 代表…… **a**

---

09 Natural Resources 自然資源

自然資源就是來自大自然的可用資源。
大自然充滿人們隨手可用的資源。
土地、水和空氣皆是重要的自然資源。

我們使用自然資源製造食品和能源。
我們需要水來飲用，需要空氣來呼吸。
我們需要土地和土壤來種植食物。
煤炭、石油和天然氣都被用來製造能源。
這些能源讓我們能駕駛車輛，也提供家庭所需的電力。

我們也從自然資源中製造許多物品。
我們用棉花和動物的羊毛去製作衣物。
我們用樹木蓋房子，做許多實用的日常用品。
石塊可以用來砌牆和蓋大樓。

- **Main Idea and Details**

1 (a)　　2 (c)　　3 (a)

4 a. **in nature**　　b. **water**

　　c. **cotton and wool from animals**

5 a. **breathe**　　b. **coal**　　c. **clothes**

- **Vocabulary Builder**

1 **natural resources** 天然資源；自然資源　2 **energy** 能源；能量

3 **electricity** 電；電流；電力　　4 **be ready**
　　　　　　　　　　　　　　　現成的；現有的；立即可得到的

---

10 Caring for Our Resources 保護自然資源

我們每天都會使用自然資源，
所以我們必須小心避免將它們耗盡，
如果我們不節約使用自然資源，
在未來我們可能沒有足夠的資源可用。

其中一種保存資源的方式是重複利用。
盡可能重複使用紙張、袋子和箱子。

另一種節約能源的方式是減少消耗資源。
試著去減少你所使用的能源量。
你可以外出時把燈關掉，
可以在刷牙時關水龍頭。

你也可以重複利用一些材料。
回收再利用就是將舊的物品製成新的東西。
收集舊物品，並將它們放進資源回收桶裡。
當我們回收某樣東西，我們可以不斷地使用它。

- **Main Idea and Details**

1 (b)　　2 (a)　　3 (c)

4 a. **conserve**　　b. **off**　　c. **recycling**

5 a. **paper**　　b. **water**　　c. **recycling bins**

- **Vocabulary Builder**

1 **conserve** 保存；保護；節省　2 **reduce** 減少；降低

3 **turn off** 關掉　　　　　　4 **recycle** 使再循環；再利用

11 Native Americans 美國原住民

美國原住民是美國最早的居民，
他們也被稱做美國印地安人。

美國原住民的祖先來自亞洲。
隨著時間過去，這些人形成了自己的部落。
他們有屬於自己的語言和習俗。
有些部落以打獵維生，
其他部落則靠著種植玉米和豆類生活。

美國原住民有許多不同形式的居所。
拉科塔族住在圓錐形帳篷；
普韋布洛族住在泥磚方形住屋；
依洛郭亦族人住在長屋裡。

美國原住民會自製使用的物品和衣著，
他們自己製作獨木舟、籃子、陶器和許多其他的手工藝品。

今日，美國原住民仍然居住在美國各處。
他們仍依循祖先的傳統過活。

• Main Idea and Details
1 **(a)**　　2 **(b)**　　3 **(c)**　　4 **(b)**
5 a. **food**　　b. **adobe**　　c. **craftworks**　　d. **traditions**

• Vocabulary Builder
1 **Native American** 美國原住民　2 **ancestor** 祖宗；祖先
3 **tribe** 部落；種族　　　　4 **custom** 習慣；風俗；習俗

12 Early American Empires 早期美洲帝國

美洲有許多部落，
有些部落建立了自己的帝國，
這三個美洲帝國分別是瑪雅帝國、阿茲提克帝國和印加帝國。

瑪雅人居住在中美洲的叢林裡，
他們用神廟和皇宮建造了雄偉的城市。
瑪雅文明非常先進，
瑪雅人已知如何寫字，
他們也有進步的數學和建築技術。
如同其他古代民族，瑪雅人尊崇許多大自然的神祇。

阿茲提克人居於現今的墨西哥，
他們在湖中島嶼建造他們的城市。
阿茲提克人是個尚武的民族，
他們征服了許多周遭民族。
他們為了崇拜太陽神建造了宏偉的石造神殿。

印加民族住在南美的安地斯山區。
他們的城市，像是馬丘比丘古城，皆座落於高山上。
印加民族建造了十分壯觀的石牆。

• Main Idea and Details
1 **(a)**　　2 **(c)**　　3 **(b)**
4 a. **empires**　　b. **warlike**　　c. **Machu Picchu**
5 a. **nature gods**　　b. **Mexico**　　c. **Andes**　　d. **Machu Picchu**

• Vocabulary Builder
1 **civilization** 文明；文明國家　2 **worship** 崇拜；敬仰
3 **nature gods** 自然神　　　　4 **warlike** 好戰的；尚武的；
　　　　　　　　　　　　　　　　　英勇的

Vocabulary Review 3

A　1 useful　　　　　　2 energy
　　3 natural gas　　　4 wool
　　5 use up　　　　　6 reuse
　　7 less　　　　　　8 recycle

B　1 American Indians　2 ancestors
　　3 tribes　　　　　4 homes
　　5 Inca　　　　　　6 jungles
　　7 modern-day　　　8 Andes

C　1 natural resources 天然資源；自然資源
　　2 electricity 電；電流；電力
　　3 recycle 使再循環；再利用　4 Native American 美國原住民
　　5 nature gods 自然神　　　6 warlike 好戰的；尚武的

D　1 能源；能量 h　　　2 現成的；現有的；
　　　　　　　　　　　　　立即可得到的 a
　　3 保存；保護；節省 d　4 減少；縮小；降低 c
　　5 關掉 b　　　　　　6 祖宗；祖先 g
　　7 部落；種族 e　　　8 習慣；風俗；習俗 j
　　9 文明；文明國家 f　　10 崇拜；敬仰 i

Wrap-Up Test 1

A　1 look after　　　　2 populations
　　3 leader　　　　　4 job
　　5 Volunteers　　　6 natural resources
　　7 off　　　　　　8 Native Americans
　　9 craftworks　　　10 worshipped

B　1 勇氣　　　　　　2 城市的
　　3 農村的；田園的　4 運輸工具；交通車輛
　　5 公民權；公民(或市民)身分　6 公正；公平
　　7 忠誠；忠心　　　8 需要；需求
　　9 放棄；讓出　　　10 非暴力
　　11 商品；貨物　　　12 洪水；水災
　　13 地圖索引　　　14 羅盤玫瑰
　　15 賺錢；掙錢　　　16 遊民收容所
　　17 位置；場所；所在地　18 方向；方位
　　19 地圖比例尺；地圖縮尺　20 代表……
　　21 天然資源；自然資源　22 電；電流；電力
　　23 使再循環；再利用　24 攻取；戰勝；征服
　　25 現成的；現有的　26 保存；保護；節省
　　27 減少；縮小；降低　28 祖宗；祖先
　　29 習慣；風俗；習俗　30 文明；文明國家

13 What Are Living Things? 何謂生物？

地球上的所有東西不是生物就是非生物。
動物和植物是生物，
生物需要食物、水和空氣來維生。
生物會成長和改變，
他們也夠繁衍如自己種族的新生命。

水、空氣和石頭是非生物。
非生物不需要食物、水和空氣。
非生物不會成長或改變。
它們無法繁衍與本身相似的新物體。

生物需要有庇護所。
庇護所是能夠安全生活的地點。
它保護生物免於受到環境和其他動物的威脅。
生物也必須有空間成長和活動。
有些生物，如花朵，只需要很小的空間。
其他生物，如大象，就需要很大的空間。

• Main Idea and Details
1 (c)   2 (b)   3 (c)
4 a. living   b. new   c. Shelter
5 a. Animals   b. living things   c. grow

• Vocabulary Builder
1 living 有生命的；活著的
2 nonliving 無生命的；死的
3 shelter 遮蓋物；躲避處；避難所
4 environment 環境；四周狀況

14 How Do Living Things Survive in the Cold? 生物如何存活在寒冷的環境？

地球上最寒冷的地方是南極洲。
南極的溫度永遠低於零度，
但是仍然有很多動物居住在那裡。
牠們如何在這麼冷的氣候下生存呢？

南極動物的身體能適應當地的寒冷。
南極的海豹和鯨魚有很多層脂肪，
這些脂肪幫助牠們保暖，
企鵝能保暖是因為牠們有小且厚的羽毛。

有些植物和動物居住在北極的凍原。
許多凍原動物有厚毛保暖。
凍原裡的植物長得不高，
它們以群聚方式靠近地面生長，
這樣能幫助它們不受寒流和強風侵襲。

人類呢？
人類的衣物具有如動物毛皮般的保暖功能。

• Main Idea and Details
1 (c)   2 (a)   3 (a)   4 (b)
5 a. feathers   b. fur   c. ground   d. clothing

• Vocabulary Builder
1 survive 倖存；活下來   2 adapt 使適應；使適合
3 Antarctica 南極洲   4 Arctic 北極的

15 How Do Plants Grow and Change? 植物如何生長和改變？

每種生物都有其生命週期。
生命週期顯示生物如何成長、生活和死亡。

植物的生命週期由種子開始，
當一顆種子由土壤獲得水和養分後，它就開始發芽。
然後，種子萌芽後，長為成熟的植物。
發育成熟的植物再次製造種子，新的生命週期再度開始。

碗豆的生命週期
讓我們來仔細看看碗豆的生命週期吧！
1. 碗豆種子被種入土壤，接受灌溉。
2. 大約一週時，種子發芽，根部加往下延伸。
3. 接著，一週後，種子變成豆芽並發育為幼苗。
4. 六週後，豆類植物成熟。
5. 花開並接受授粉後，長出碗豆。

• Main Idea and Details
1 (a)   2 (b)   3 (c)
4 a. water and nutrients from the soil
   b. Its roots grow down.
   c. flowers that get fertilized
5 a. water   b. seedling   c. fertilized   d. seeds

• Vocabulary Builder
1 life cycle 生命週期   2 germinate 發芽；生長
3 sprout 發芽；很快地成長   4 seedling 幼苗；秧苗

16 How Do Plants Survive in the Desert? 植物如何在沙漠裡生存？

植物幾乎在任何地方都可以生長，
有些植物甚至長在沙漠裡。
沙漠的生長環境非常惡劣，
沙漠的天氣非常炎熱乾燥，雨水稀少。
只有極少數的植物和動物適應沙漠生活。
然而，有些植物，像仙人掌，就能在沙漠裡生長得很好。
它們是如何在這麼乾燥的環境下生存呢？

仙人掌有厚實的莖和針狀的葉，
這些莖和葉能幫助仙人掌儲藏水分，
等它日後需要水分時就能運用。
因此，仙人掌可以在無雨的狀態生存很長的時間。

仙人掌的根從它本身往外散布，
這些根也離地面很近，
使根部在降雨時吸取大量雨水。

• Main Idea and Details
1 (b)   2 (a)   3 (c)
4 a. Deserts   b. water   c. roots
5 a. adapted   b. store   c. ground   d. capture

1 **harsh** 嚴酷的；惡劣的　　2 **spiny** 多刺的；尖刺狀的
3 **store** 儲存；儲藏　　4 **spread out** 攤開；散開

Vocabulary Review 4

A　1 **living things**　　2 **air**
　　3 **nonliving things**　　4 **environment**
　　5 **coldest**　　6 **manage to**
　　7 **adapted**　　8 **fur**

B　1 **life cycle**　　2 **seed**
　　3 **nutrients**　　4 **fertilized**
　　5 **harsh**　　6 **cactus**
　　7 **thick**　　8 **away**

C　1 **living** 有生命的；活著的　　2 **nonliving** 無生命的；死的
　　3 **germinate** 發芽；生長　　4 **seedling** 幼苗；秧苗
　　5 **Antarctica** 南極洲　　6 **spiny** 多刺的；尖刺狀的

D　1 環境；四周狀況 i　　2 遮蓋物；躲避處；避難所 b
　　3 倖存；活下來 a　　4 使適應；使適合 j
　　5 北極的 e　　6 發芽；很快地成長 c
　　7 生命週期 h　　8 嚴酷的；惡劣的 f
　　9 儲存；儲藏 g　　10 攤開；散開 d

17　Kinds of Animals 動物的種類

你知道貓、獅子和海豚的相同點是什麼嗎？
牠們全都是哺乳動物。
哺乳動物是有毛皮或毛髮的動物，
大多數的哺乳動物會分娩繁殖下一代。
哺乳動物以母乳來餵食幼兒。

鳥類有喙狀的嘴、羽毛、翅膀和足。
大部分的鳥類用翅膀飛行。
鳥類會下蛋，幼鳥會由蛋中孵出。
鴨子、孔雀和企鵝都是鳥類。

爬蟲類有乾燥的皮膚，上頭覆蓋著鱗片。
大多數的爬蟲類會下蛋並用四隻腳行走。
蛇、烏龜和鱷魚都屬於爬蟲類。

兩棲類可生活在陸地和水中。
大多數的兩棲類有著平滑、潮濕的皮膚，也會下蛋。
青蛙和蠑螈都屬於兩棲類。

魚類住在水中。
大多數的魚類有魚鱗、魚鰭和魚鰓。
牠們會產卵，神仙魚和鯊魚都屬於魚類。

• Main Idea and Details
1 (c)　　2 (a)　　3 (b)　　4 (b)
5 a. **young**　b. **wings**　c. **scales**　d. **water**　e. **gills**
• Vocabulary Builder
1 **mammals** 哺乳動物　　2 **young** 幼小動物；幼禽總稱
3 **amphibians** 兩棲動物　　4 **reptiles** 爬行動物；爬蟲類

18　Insects 昆蟲知多少

昆蟲種類有上百萬種，
包括螞蟻、蝴蝶、蜜蜂和蟋蟀。

許多昆蟲看起來互不相同，
但牠們其實都有許多相似處，
所有的昆蟲都有三大身體結構和六隻腳。
多數的昆蟲會產卵。

讓我們來仔細看看昆蟲的三大身體結構：
頭部、胸部和腹部。
頭部有昆蟲的眼睛、觸角和口器，
昆蟲用觸角來產生觸覺。
胸部有足肢和翅膀。
所有的昆蟲都有三對足肢，
但並不是所有昆蟲都有翅膀。
腹部通常是昆蟲最大的身體結構，
雌性昆蟲由腹部產卵，
蜜蜂這類昆蟲的螫針也在腹部。

• Main Idea and Details
1 (b)　　2 (c)　　3 (c)
4 a. **the head, thorax, and abdomen**
　b. **the legs and wings**　c. **stingers**
5 a. **antennae**　b. **pairs**　c. **largest**　d. **stingers**
• Vocabulary Builder
1 **thorax** （昆蟲的）胸部　　2 **abdomen** 腹；下腹；腹部
3 **antennae** （動物的）觸角；觸鬚
4 **stinger** （昆蟲的）螫針；刺

19　The Life Cycle of an Animal 動物的生命週期

動物如何成長和改變？
所有動物都有生命週期。
生命週期是動物一生會經過的所有成長階段。
大多數的動物會經過四個階段：出生、成長、繁衍和死亡。

當哺乳動物出生時，牠們是無助的，
牠們看不見，也無法行走，
牠們的母親必須照顧牠們，直到牠們能照顧自己。

當哺乳動物長大，牠們的容貌開始與父母相似。
貓和狗需要約一年的時間才算成年。
人類需要超過十年的時間才能成熟。
當哺乳動物成年後，就可以繁衍後代，
然後牠們可以育有與牠們面貌相似的後代。

最後，最終階段是死亡。
當哺乳動物走到生命的終點時，牠們就會死亡。

• Main Idea and Details
1 (a)　　2 (b)　　3 (a)
4 a. **stages**　b. **birth**　c. **parents**
5 a. **care**　b. **mature**　c. **young**　d. **end**

• Vocabulary Builder
1 **growth** 生長;成長;發育　　2 **reproduction** 生殖;繁育

3 **go through** 經歷　　4 **take care of** 照顧

20 The Life Cycle of a Frog 青蛙的生命週期

青蛙是兩棲類,
牠們的生命週期與哺乳動物不同。
事實上,青蛙的生命週期相當獨特。

青蛙會在春季於水中產卵,
大約兩週後,蝌蚪由卵中孵化。
事實上,蝌蚪完全不像青蛙。
牠們沒有腳,但有尾巴。
蝌蚪也有腮,
牠們用腮在水中呼吸和生活。

當蝌蚪長大,牠們就準備要到陸地上生活。
牠們發展出腳,尾巴也變得較短。
同時,牠們長出肺部,以便在陸地上呼吸。
之後,蝌蚪便開始長得像青蛙了。
大約14週後,青蛙成為成蛙,尾巴消失。
牠們移居岸上,並大多生活在該處。

• Main Idea and Details

1 **(c)**　　2 **(b)**　　3 **(b)**　　4 **(c)**

5 a. **tail**　　b. **legs**　　c. **lungs**

• Vocabulary Builder

1 **tadpole** 蝌蚪　　2 **hatch** 孵出

3 **resemble** 像;類似　　4 **lungs** 肺;肺臟

Vocabulary Review 5

A 1 **common**　　2 **give birth to**

3 **feed**　　4 **lay eggs**

5 **species**　　6 **legs**

7 **antennae**　　8 **wings**

B 1 **change**　　2 **stages**

3 **helpless**　　4 **reproduce**

5 **unique**　　6 **hatch**

7 **grow older**　　8 **develop**

C 1 **mammals** 哺乳動物　　2 **young** 幼小動物;幼禽總稱

3 **amphibians** 兩棲動物　　4 **reptiles** 爬行動物;爬蟲類

5 **thorax** (昆蟲的)胸部　　6 **tadpole** 蝌蚪

D 1 腹;下腹;腹部 **j**　　2 (動物的)觸角;觸鬚 **i**

3 (昆蟲的)螫針;刺 **h**　　4 生長;成長;發育 **d**

5 生殖;繁育 **f**　　6 經歷 **b**

7 照顧 **a**　　8 孵出 **c**

9 像;類似 **e**　　10 肺;肺臟 **g**

21 What Are Food Chains? 何謂食物鏈?

動物需要依賴食物來維生,
食物供給牠們能量來存活。
不同的動物會吃不同的食物,
有的動物以植物為食,有的則吃其他動物。

食物鏈顯示動物吃植物和其他動物的順序。
在食物鏈的最底端是植物,
太陽供給植物能量,
以植物為食的動物在下一個鏈,
我們稱之為草食性動物。
草食性動物通常是小型昆蟲,像是蚱蜢。
松鼠和兔子也是草食性動物,
以其他動物為食的動物是第三個鏈,
我們稱之為肉食性動物。
牠們可能是小型動物,如青蛙和蛇類。
然後更大型的動物,像貓頭鷹和熊類吃這些小型動物。

不會被獵食的動物在食物鏈的頂端。
事實上,人類即是在許多食物鏈的最頂端。

• Main Idea and Details

1 **(c)**　　2 **(a)**　　3 **(b)**

4 a. **small insects or animals like grasshopper, squirrels, and rabbits**

　　b. **animals that eat other animals**

　　c. **animals that are not hunted by other animals / people**

5 a. **energy**　　b. **insects**　　c. **Frogs**　　d. **hunted**

• Vocabulary Builder

1 **food chain** 食物鏈　　2 **meat eaters** 肉食性動物

3 **order** 順序;次序　　4 **link** (鏈狀物的)環;節

22 The Ocean Food Chain 海洋食物鏈

食物鏈也存在於海洋中。
海洋是個充滿生命的地方,
在海洋食物鏈中,這些生命形式不是以其他生物為主食,
就是被其他生物所吃。

海藻是海洋食物鏈的最底層,
它們藉由陽光製造食物。
小型的生物,如浮游生物,以海藻為食。
接著,稍大一些的生物以浮游生物為食,
通常是有殼類生物,像蛤蜊、蝦和蟹。
小型魚類吃有殼類生物,
例如鱈魚、青魚和比目魚。
接著,大魚再吃小魚,
鮪魚、劍魚和鯊魚都是大魚。

最後,殺人鯨和大白鯊以大魚為主食,
牠們位於食物鏈的最頂端。

- Main Idea and Details

1 (a)　　　2 (b)　　　3 (b)

4 a. **shellfish**　　b. **Algae**　　c. **top**

5 a. **light**　　b. **Plankton**　　c. **sharks**　　d. **Killer whales**

- Vocabulary Builder

1 **algae** 水藻；海藻　　　　2 **creature** 生物；動物

3 **shellfish** 貝；有殼的水生動物 4 **consume** 消耗；花費

23 What Is the Solar System?
太陽系知多少

我們都生活在地球上，
地球是一個大型系統的一部分，稱為太陽系。

太陽系由太陽和其他行星組成。
行星是繞行太陽的大型星體。
太陽系有八個行星，
地球是繞行太陽的八個行星之一，
以太陽為基準點依序來說，這八個行星分別是：水星、金星、
地球、火星、木星、土星、天王星和海王星。

太陽位於太陽系的中心。
這八個行星沿著路徑繞行太陽，
每條路徑叫做軌道。

這些行星都不太一樣，
有些行星比地球小，有些行星比地球大。
它們看起來互不相同，與太陽的距離也相異。

- Main Idea and Details

1 (b)　　　2 (c)　　　3 (c)　　　4 (a)

5 a. **center**　　b. **Saturn**　　c. **distances**

- Vocabulary Builder

1 **solar system** 太陽系　　　2 **planet** 行星

3 **path** 路線；軌道　　　　4 **orbit** （天體等的）運行軌道

24 What Causes the Seasons?
季節的形成

一年有四個季節：春季、夏季、秋季和冬季。
一年當中，四季更迭，
是什麼造成季節的改變呢？

地球繞著太陽公轉的同時也每日自轉，
地球需要花上一年才能繞太陽一圈。

地球總是往同一方向傾斜，
當地球繞著太陽運行，向太陽傾斜的那一面也會跟著改變，
造成四季的變化。
當你居住的地點朝太陽的方向傾斜，太陽光會直射該區域，
形成夏天；
當你居住的地點遠離太陽的方向傾斜，就變成了冬天。
這樣的模式每年都會重覆。

- Main Idea and Details

1 (a)　　　2 (c)　　　3 (c)

4 a. **seasons**　　b. **direction**　　c. **winter**

5 a. **fall**　　b. **tilted**　　c. **toward**　　d. **away**

- Vocabulary Builder

1 **tilt** 使傾斜；使偏斜　　　2 **rotate** 旋轉；轉動

3 **cause** 導致；使發生；引起　　4 **complete** 完成；結束

Vocabulary Review 6

A　1 plants　　　　　　2 plant eaters
　　3 animals　　　　　4 hunted
　　5 ocean　　　　　　6 plankton
　　7 killer whales　　　8 top

B　1 system　　　　　2 object
　　3 Saturn　　　　　4 planets
　　5 throughout　　　6 complete
　　7 direction　　　　8 away

C　1 food chain 食物鏈　　2 meat eaters 肉食性動物
　　3 shellfish 貝；有殼的　　4 solar system 太陽系
　　　　水生動物
　　5 tilt 傾斜；偏斜　　　6 algae 水藻；海藻

D　1 順序；次序 c　　　　2 （鏈狀物的）環；節 a
　　3 生物；動物 b　　　　4 消耗；花費 g
　　5 行星 h　　　　　　6 路線；軌道 i
　　7 （天體等的）運行軌道 j　8 旋轉；轉動 d
　　9 導致；使發生；引起 f　10 完成；結束 e

Wrap-Up Test 2

A　1 nonliving　　　　2 abdomen
　　3 survive　　　　　4 stay warm
　　5 reptile　　　　　6 go through
　　7 food chain　　　8 creatures
　　9 planets　　　　10 seasons

B　1 有生命的；活著的　　2 發芽；生長
　　3 幼苗；秧苗　　　　4 環境；四周狀況
　　5 遮蓋物；躲藏處；避難所　6 使適應；使適合
　　7 攤開；散開　　　　8 哺乳動物
　　9 兩棲動物　　　　10 爬行動物；爬蟲類
　　11 腹；下腹；腹部　　12 （動物的）觸角；觸鬚
　　13 （昆蟲的）螫針；刺　14 生殖；繁育
　　15 照顧　　　　　　16 孵出
　　17 像；類似　　　　18 食物鏈
　　19 順序；次序　　　20 （鏈狀物的）環；節
　　21 生物；動物　　　22 消耗；花費
　　23 行星　　　　　　24 路線；軌道
　　25 （天體等的）運行軌道　26 旋轉；轉動
　　27 導致；使發生；引起　28 完成；結束
　　29 太陽系　　　　　30 傾斜；偏斜

25 Addition and Subtraction 加法和減法運算

加法就是將兩個以上的數字相加。
假設有三隻螞蟻在一片樹葉上，然後又有四隻加入，
那麼現在共有幾隻螞蟻呢？
3 + 4 = 7
共有七隻螞蟻。
將這些數目相加後所得到的答案叫做「總和」。
因此，你可以說「3 + 4的總和是7」。
或是，你也可以說「三加四等於七」。

減法就是將某數字去掉一個數目。
假設你的朋友有五塊餅乾，
你肚子餓了，所以拿走兩塊。
那麼還剩下幾塊餅乾呢？
5 − 2 = 3
還剩下三塊餅乾。
你減去的數字後剩下的數字叫做「差」。
因此，你可以說「5 - 2的差是3」。
或者，你也可以說「五減二等於三」。

- **Main Idea and Details**
1 **(b)**　　2 **(a)**　　3 **(b)**
4 a. **addition**　　b. **equals**　　c. **minus**
5 a. **sum**　　b. **away**　　c. **difference**
- **Vocabulary Builder**
1 **subtraction** 減；減算　　2 **plus (+)** 加；加上
3 **minus (−)** 減；減去　　4 **equals (=)** 等於

26 Counting Money 數錢

我們用錢來購物。
錢有分硬幣跟紙鈔，
所有鈔票的面值都不相同。

美元有數種不同的硬幣和鈔票。
1美分硬幣（penny）面值為1美分。1美分硬幣 = 1美分
（¢ 為美分的符號）
5美分硬幣（nickel）面值為5美分。5美分硬幣 = 5美分
10美分硬幣（dime）面值為10美分。10美分硬幣 = 10美分
25美分硬幣（quarter）面值為25美分。25美分硬幣 = 25美分
半美元（half-dollar）面值為50美分。半美元 = 50美分
一美元硬幣的面值等於一百美分。
1美元 = 100 美分

鈔票的面值有：
1元、2元、5元、10元、20元、50元和100元。

我們常把錢的數目寫成：$1.50。
以$1.50來說，我們可以說成「一元五十分」。
因此，$25.20就是「二十五元二十分」。

- **Main Idea and Details**
1 **(c)**　　2 **(c)**　　3 **(b)**　　4 **(c)**
5 a. **Nickel**　　b. **Quarter**　　c. **Half-dollar**　　d. **values**

- **Vocabulary Builder**
1 **be worth** 有……的價值；值……　　2 **penny** 一分；一分硬幣
3 **dime** 一角硬幣　　4 **half-dollar** 五角銀幣

27 Telling Time 表達時間

時鐘有兩個指針：短針和長針。
短針表示小時，
因此，也可以叫它做時針。
長針表示分鐘，
因此，也可以叫它做分針。

我們是怎麼表達時間的呢？
很簡單，只要讀出小時然後再讀分鐘就行了。
所以2:10就是「兩點十分」。
5:25就是「五點二十五分」。

有時候，時間如果是4:30，
我們會說「四點三十分」或是「四點半」。
同樣地，7:15我們可以說「七點十五」或是「七點又十五
分」。
9:45可以說成「九點四十五分」或是「再十五分鐘就十點」。

當長針指向12，短針指向6的時候。
時間就是6點，我們可以寫成6:00。
6:00的意思與6點相同。

- **Main Idea and Details**
1 **(a)**　　2 **(b)**　　3 **(a)**
4 a. **two**　　b. **"four fifteen" or "fifteen minutes after four"**
　　c. **"four forty-five" or "fifteen minutes before five"**
5 a. **hour**　　b. **minute**　　c. **half**　　d. **before**
- **Vocabulary Builder**
1 **hour hand** 時針　　2 **minute hand** 分針
3 **half** 一半；二分之一　　4 **the same as** 與……相同

28 Reading a Calendar 看月曆

我們可以用月曆或時鐘來計算時間。
月曆顯示日期、星期和月分。

讓我們來看看月曆。
在第一頁，它顯示一月。
一月是一年的第一個月。
一年有十二個月。
有一月、二月、三月、四月、五月、六月、七月、八月。
九月、十月、十一月和十二月。
所以月曆總共有十二頁。

在每一頁，有四或五排數字。
每個數字代表這個月的日期。
一星期有七天。
有星期天、星期一、星期二、星期三、星期四、
星期五和星期六。
每一排代表一個星期。
每個月有大約四個星期。

- **Main Idea and Details**

1 **(b)**　　2 **(b)**　　3 **(c)**

4 a. **January**　　b. **weeks**　　c. **days**

5 a. **twelve(12)**　　b. **December**　　c. **seven(7)**　　d. **four(4)**

- **Vocabulary Builder**

1 **calendar** 日曆　　2 **week** 週；一星期

3 **represent** 象徵；表示　　4 **row** 列；排

Vocabulary Review 7

A　1 adding　　2 sum

　　3 taking　　4 difference

　　5 equals　　6 coins

　　7 worth　　8 quarter

B　1 hands　　2 hour

　　3 half　　4 before

　　5 days　　6 January

　　7 represents　　8 month

C　1 **subtraction** 減；減算　　2 **plus (+)** 加；加上

　　3 **penny** 一分錢　　4 **dime** 一角硬幣

　　5 **minute hand** 分針　　6 **calendar** 日曆

D　1 減（去）**i**　　2 等於 **j**

　　3 有……的價值；值…… **c**　　4 五角銀幣 **e**

　　5 時針 **d**　　6 一半；二分之一 **f**

　　7 與……相同 **a**　　8 週；一星期 **g**

　　9 象徵；表示 **b**　　10 列；排 **h**

---

29 Parts of Speech 詞類

每個句子都有一個主詞和一個動詞。

　　湯姆跑得很快。　　她吃披薩。

在上述的句子裡，「湯姆」和「她」是主詞，

「跑」和「吃」是動詞。

主詞通常是名詞。

主詞指稱一個人物、地點或東西。

動詞描述句子裡的動作。

「唱歌」、「跳舞」、「微笑」和「大笑」都是動詞。

名詞和動詞是句子裡最重要的詞類。

我們也會使用其他詞類。

代名詞是像「我」、「他」、「她」、「它」、「我們」、

「你們」和「他們」這些詞。我們用代名詞來代替名詞。

形容詞可以形容名詞和代名詞，

　　一隻可愛的狗　一個高個兒男孩　一隻快樂的貓

「可愛」、「高個兒」和「快樂」都是形容詞。

副詞用來形容動詞。

　　他突然哭泣。　她緩慢地走。

介係詞常幫助我們了解位置。

例如「in 在……裡面」、「on 在……上方」、「under

在……之下」、「above 在……之上」和「by 在……旁

邊」。

- **Main Idea and Details**

1 **(b)**　　2 **(b)**　　3 **(a)**　　4 **(a)**

5 a. **place**　　b. **action**　　c. **place of**

　　d. **Describes**　　e. **location**

- **Vocabulary Builder**

1 **describe** 描寫；描繪；敘述　　2 **adjective** 形容詞

3 **adverb** 副詞　　4 **preposition** 介係詞

---

30 Contractions and Abbreviations 縮略語和縮寫字

當我們書寫時，我們常會將兩個字結合成一個比較短的字。

這個比較短的字就叫做縮約字。

當我們要寫一個縮約字，我們會在兩個字中間放一個省略符號

「'」，比方說：

　　I am = I'm　　　you are = you're　　it is = it's

　　do not = don't　　cannot = can't　　is not = isn't

有些字可被縮短或簡約。

許多縮寫詞會以大寫字母起首，以句點結束。

星期的名稱通常會以縮寫呈現。

　　Monday = Mon.　　Tuesday = Tue.　　Wednesday = Wed.

　　Thursday = Thur.　　Friday = Fri.　　Saturday = Sat.

　　Sunday = Sun.

月分通常會如此縮寫。

　　January = Jan.　　February = Feb.　　March = Mar.

　　April = Apr.　　August = Aug.　　September = Sept.

　　October = Oct.　　November = Nov.　　December = Dec.

五月、六月和七月不使用縮寫式。

人的稱謂和街道名也常使用縮寫。

　　Mister = Mr.　　Professor = Prof.　　Doctor = Dr.

　　Street = St.　　Avenue = Ave.　　Road = Rd.

- **Main Idea and Details**

1 **(a)**　　2 **(b)**　　3 **(a)**

4 a. **I'm**　　b. **Sun.**　　c. **doctor**

5 a. **apostrophe**　　b. **capital**　　c. **period**

- **Vocabulary Builder**

1 **contraction** 縮略語／縮略字

2 **abbreviation** 縮寫字；縮寫式

3 **shorten** 使變短；縮短　　4 **abbreviate** 縮寫；省略

31 Types of Writing 寫作的形式

有很多不同的寫作形式，
你能舉出幾種寫作形式的名稱嗎？

詩是一種使用韻腳的短篇文章。
它通常會在句尾重複相同的韻腳，例如冷「酷」和抓「住」。
童話是為孩童寫的故事，充滿魔幻的情節。
寓言是含有道德教育的短篇故事，
在許多寓言裡，動物會像人一樣說話和動作。
小說是虛構的長篇故事，
小說裡時常充滿各種角色。

傳記是一個人真實的人生故事，
自傳是作者本人親自寫的傳記。

虛構小說不是真實發生的故事，例如童話故事或長篇小說。
當你編撰一則故事，你正在創作小說。
非小說類是關於事實或真實事件的文章。
傳記和自傳就是非小說。

• **Main Idea and Details**

1 (c)   2 (b)   3 (b)
4 a. **novel**   b. **biography**   c. **fiction**
5 a. **rhymes**   b. **Novel**   c. **facts**   d. **Autobiography**

• **Vocabulary Builder**

1 **poem** 詩   2 **biography** 傳記
3 **fiction** （總稱）小說   4 **nonfiction** 非小說類

32 The Emperor's New Clothes 《國王的新衣》

很久很久以前，有一位很愛打扮的國王。
他每天都會穿著最漂亮的衣服，到處去炫耀一番。

有一天，有兩個騙子進城來，他們告訴國王說他們能織出世界
上最美麗的布。他們說：「我們能織出具有魔力的布，只有聰
明的人才看得見。」國王付給他們一大筆錢，並命令他們馬上
動手織布。

這兩個騙子日以繼夜地假裝織起布來，可是織布機上什麼也沒
有。國王到裁縫室想一探究竟，卻看不到任何的布。
他心想：「這真是太糟糕了！難道我是個愚笨的人嗎？」
但他卻大聲地說：「這塊布簡直巧奪天工啊！」

終於，到了國王穿新衣服參加遊行的那天。國王穿著他的內
衣，驕傲地一路走著！街上的人群看見，紛紛說：「這真是件
華麗的衣裳啊！」
沒人敢承認他根本沒看到任何東西。
然而，到最後，只見人群中一個小孩大聲叫喊：「國王什麼衣
服也沒穿呀！」

• **Main Idea and Details**

1 (a)   2 (a)   3 (c)   4 (b)
5 a. **magic**   b. **emperor's**   c. **clothes**   d. **underclothes**

• Vocabulary Builder

1 **emperor** 皇帝；國王   2 **thief** 賊；小偷
3 **weave** 織；編   4 **underclothes** 內衣；襯衣

Vocabulary Review 8

A 1 **subject**   2 **parts of speech**
   3 **describe**   4 **Prepositions**
   5 **combine**   6 **apostrophe**
   7 **shortened**   8 **abbreviated**

B 1 **writing**   2 **rhymes**
   3 **fairy tale**   4 **fiction**
   5 **clothes**   6 **showed off**
   7 **pretended**   8 **proudly**

C 1 **adjective** 形容詞   2 **adverb** 副詞
   3 **contraction** 略語
   4 **abbreviation** 縮寫字；縮寫式
   5 **nonfiction** 非小說類的寫實文學作品
   6 **emperor** 皇帝；國王

D 1 描寫；描繪；敘述 i   2 介係詞 g
   3 使變短；縮短 c   4 縮寫；省略 a
   5 詩 e   6 傳記 f
   7 小說 h   8 賊；小偷 d
   9 織；編 b   10 內衣；襯衣 j

33 A World of Colors 彩色的世界

環顧四周，
你可以看見許多不同的顏色，
它們有些是亮色系，有些是深色系。

所有顏色都從三原色而來。
這三原色是紅色、黃色和藍色。

這三種原色可以讓我們創造出其他色彩。
要怎麼做呢？
我們只要混合兩種原色就可以了，
我們可以混合紅色和黃色成為橘色；
我們可以混合紅色和藍色成為紫色；
我們也可以混合藍色和黃色成為綠色。
橘色、紫色和綠色是三種三間色。

在繪畫裡，原色和三間色很重要。
藉由混合不同份量的三間色，我們可創出世界上任何色彩。

• **Main Idea and Details**

1 (a)   2 (b)   3 (c)
4 a. **red, yellow, and blue**   b. **orange**
   c. **They are secondary colors.**
5 a. **yellow**   b. **purple**   c. **primary**

• Vocabulary Builder

1 **primary colors** 原色   2 **secondary colors** 第二次色
3 **mix** 混合；混入   4 **combine** 結合；聯合

34 Lines and Shapes 線條和形狀

我們通常會使用線條來作畫。
線條有很多種形式：直線、曲線、曲折線、波形線和螺旋形線。

—— 直線	⌒ 曲線	〰 曲折線
〰〰 波浪線	◉ 螺旋形線	

線條也分為細線和粗線。

—— 細線	━━ 粗線

上下筆直的線條叫做垂直線。
左右筆直的線條叫做水平線。
上下傾斜某個角度的線條叫做對角線。

│	──	╱
垂直線	水平線	對角線

你能看出它們的相異之處嗎？

當線條連在一起時，會成為形狀。
有三種基本形狀：方形、圓形和三角形。
方形由四條直線構成。 □
圓形由單一曲線構成。 ○
三角形由三條直線構成。 △

• Main Idea and Details
1 (b)　　2 (c)　　3 (a)
4 a. Lines　　b. right　　c. curved
5 a. wavy　　b. Horizontal　　c. lines　　d. straight

• Vocabulary Builder
1 curved 彎曲的　　2 wavy 波浪形的
3 spiral 螺旋形的　　4 form 形成

35 Musicians and Their Instruments 音樂家和他們的樂器

樂器的種類有很多，
它們分別屬於不同的樂器類別。
樂器分為打擊樂器、弦樂器、鍵盤樂器、木管樂器和銅管樂器。
管弦樂隊裡音樂家會在演奏這些樂器

鼓是打擊樂器。
鼓手打鼓。
小提琴、大提琴和吉他是弦樂器。
小提琴家、大提琴家和吉他手演奏這些樂器。
鋼琴和風琴是最常見的鍵盤樂器。
鋼琴家和風琴家演奏這些樂器。
長笛和豎笛是木管樂器。
長笛家和豎笛家演奏這些樂器。
小號和長號是兩種銅管樂器。
小號演奏家吹小號；
長號演奏家吹長號。
將所有演奏家匯聚一堂，他們就能演奏出優美的樂曲。

• Main Idea and Details
1 (c)　　2 (b)　　3 (a)　　4 (c)
5 a. drummer　b. violinist　c. clarinetist　d. trombonist
• Vocabulary Builder
1 belong to 屬於　　2 musician 音樂家
3 drummer 鼓手　　4 flutist 長笛手；吹長笛者

36 Mozart and Beethoven 莫札特與貝多芬

作曲家會寫曲、作曲。
沃夫岡・阿瑪迪斯・莫札特是世上最偉大的音樂作曲家之一。
他是音樂神童，
從很小時便開始彈鋼琴與作曲。
莫札特曾在歐洲四處巡演，
創作出許多優秀的作品。
他的作品囊括歌劇、交響樂和其他許多作品。
不幸地，他在35歲便英年早逝。

另一位偉大的作曲家是路德維希・范・貝多芬。
他和莫札特一樣四處巡演，
但他不久後就定居於維也納。
貝多芬是一位傑出的鋼琴家。
但他年約30歲時便逐漸耳聾，
然而，他依舊持續演奏和創作音樂。
他的《第九號交響曲》是世上最為人熟知的樂曲之一。

現今，人們仍會聆聽莫札特和貝多芬的樂曲。

• Main Idea and Details
1 (b)　　2 (c)　　3 (b)
4 a. child　　b. Beethoven　　c. *Ninth Symphony*
5 a. genius　　b. operas　　c. deaf　　d. compose
• Vocabulary Builder
1 composer 作曲家　　2 compose 創作（詩歌、樂曲）；為……譜曲
3 genius 天才　　4 go deaf 變聾

Vocabulary Review 9

A 1 blue　　　　　　2 mix
　　3 secondary　　　4 come in
　　5 rough　　　　　6 horizontal
　　7 diagonal　　　　8 straight

B 1 instruments　　　2 musicians
　　3 organists　　　　4 trombonist
　　5 composers　　　6 symphonies
　　7 deaf　　　　　　8 famous

C 1 primary colors 原色　　2 secondary colors 第二次色
　　3 mix 混合；混入　　　　4 spiral 螺旋形的
　　5 drummer 鼓手　　　　6 composer 作曲家

D 1 結合；聯合 **g**　　　2 彎曲的 **d**

3 波浪形的 **a**　　　　4 形成 **c**

5 屬於 **e**　　　　　　6 音樂家 **i**

7 小號手 **h**　　　　　8 作曲 **b**

9 天才 **j**　　　　　　10 變聾 **f**

Wrap-Up Test 3

A 1 Subtraction　　　　2 bills

3 same as　　　　　　4 time

5 in place of　　　　　6 abbreviations

7 nonfiction　　　　　8 weave

9 primary　　　　　　10 genius

B 1 加；加上　　　　　2 減（去）

3 等於　　　　　　　4 一分；一分硬幣

5 一角硬幣　　　　　6 分針

7 日曆　　　　　　　8 有……的價值；值……

9 五角銀幣　　　　　10 列；排

11 形容詞　　　　　　12 副詞

13 縮短；縮約；　　　14 小說
縮短形；縮約形式

15 皇帝；國王　　　　16 描寫；描繪；敘述

17 使變短；縮短　　　18 縮寫；省略

19 傳記　　　　　　　20 賊；小偷

21 原色　　　　　　　22 第二次色

23 結合；聯合　　　　24 彎曲的

25 波浪形的　　　　　26 螺旋形的

27 形成　　　　　　　28 屬於

29 音樂家　　　　　　30 作曲家

FÜN學 美國英語閱讀課本 2
各學科實用課文

Authors

Michael A. Putlack
Michael A. Putlack graduated from Tufts University in Medford, Massachusetts, USA, where he got his B.A. in History and English and his M.A. in History. He has written a number of books for children, teenagers, and adults.

e-Creative Contents
A creative group that develops English contents and products for ESL and EFL students.

作者	Michael A. Putlack & e-Creative Contents
翻譯	丁宥暄
製程管理	洪巧玲
發行人	黃朝萍
出版者	寂天文化事業股份有限公司
電話	+886-(0)2-2365-9739
傳真	+886-(0)2-2365-9835
網址	www.icosmos.com.tw
讀者服務	onlineservice@icosmos.com.tw
出版日期	2023 年 12 月 二版再刷 （寂天雲隨身聽APP版）(0204)

Copyright © 2010 by Key Publications
Photos © Jupiterimages Corporation

Copyright © 2021 by Cosmos Culture Ltd.
All rights reserved. 版權所有　請勿翻印
郵撥帳號 1998620-0　寂天文化事業股份有限公司
訂書金額未滿1000元，請外加運費100元。
〔若有破損，請寄回更換，謝謝。〕

國家圖書館出版品預行編目(CIP)資料

FUN學美國英語閱讀課本：各學科實用課文(寂天雲隨身
聽APP版) / Michael A. Putlack, e-Creative Contents著；
丁宥暄譯. -- 二版. --[臺北市]：
寂天文化, 2021.06-印刷
　冊；　公分
ISBN 978-626-300-027-8 (第2冊：菊8K平裝). --
1.英語 2.讀本
805.18　　　　　　　　　　　110010424

FUN學
美國英語閱讀課本
各學科實用課文 二版

2

Workbook

AMERICAN
SCHOOL
TEXTBOOK
READING KEY

作者 Michael A. Putlack & e-Creative Contents   譯者 丁宥暄

A Listen to the passage and fill in the blanks. 🎧 37

We live together in a _____.

How can you be a _____ citizen in your community?

There are seven ways to show good _____: caring, responsibility,

honesty, courage, _____, respect, and loyalty.

Caring means thinking about what others _____.

Good citizens _____ _____ their neighbors and care for others.

_____ means doing the things you should do.

Always try to be a _____ person.

Good citizens should be _____.

Honesty means telling the _____.

It is not always easy to do the _____ thing.

That is why a good _____ needs courage, too.

Courage means being _____ even when it is hard.

Good citizens treat others _____ and with respect.

Finally, good citizens are _____ to their friends, family, community, and country.

B Write the meaning of each word or phrase from Word List (main book p.104) in English.

1	社區；共同社會	_____	11	照料	_____
2	公民身分	_____	12	責任	_____
3	關懷；照顧	_____	13	誠實的	_____
4	責任；義務	_____	14	實話；事實	_____
5	誠實	_____	15	正確的	_____
6	膽量；勇氣	_____	16	勇敢的	_____
7	公正；公平	_____	17	對待	_____
8	尊敬	_____	18	公平地	_____
9	忠誠；忠心	_____	19	尊重地	_____
10	照顧	_____	20	忠誠的	_____

02 Different Kinds of Communities

A Listen to the passage and fill in the blanks.   🎧38

There are many different _____ of communities.

Some communities are small, and _____ are big.

An _____ community is in a city.

Many people live and work in _____.

People in cities often live in big _____ buildings.

Supermarkets, department stores, and other stores are _____ their homes.

A rural community is in the _____.

Usually, _____ areas are surrounded by land and fields.

They have small _____.

People in rural areas usually live in _____.

Shops and buildings are often located _____ from people's homes.

A _____ community is near a city.

_____ are small cities _____ near big cities.

They are like a _____ of urban and rural areas.

Most _____ are not as busy as cities.

They have _____ populations.

B Write the meaning of each word or phrase from Word List in English.

1	城市的	_____	9	位於；座落於	_____
2	公寓大樓	_____	10	遙遠的	_____
3	百貨公司	_____	11	郊區的	_____
4	農村的	_____	12	近郊住宅區	_____
5	鄉間	_____	13	像；如	_____
6	被……圍繞	_____	14	結合；聯合	_____
7	農村的	_____	15	像……那樣忙碌	_____
8	人口	_____	16	中型的	_____

03 The Leaders of Government

In the United States, each community and _____ has a leader.

People _____ their leaders.

In a community, the _____ is the leader.

The citizens of the community _____ _____ their leaders.

In a state, the governor is the _____.

The citizens of each state vote for their _____.

The _____ leads the whole country.

Every four years, the citizens _____ a president to run the country.

The leaders provide for the _____ of the people in the community, state, and country.

Some of these needs include education, safety, and _____.

Each of these leaders also _____ _____ that people follow the law.

_____ are very important.

Laws protect people and _____ them from harming others.

Laws help citizens live together in peace and _____.

B Write the meaning of each word or phrase from Word List in English.

1 領袖;領導者 _____

2 市長;鎮長 _____

3 投票 _____

4 美國州長 _____

5 領導;帶領 _____

6 選舉 _____

7 管理;指揮 _____

8 提供 _____

9 需要;需求 _____

10 教育 _____

11 安全;平安 _____

12 大眾運輸工具 _____

13 確保 _____

14 法律 _____

15 保護;防護 _____

16 阻止;制止 _____

17 損傷;傷害 _____

18 和睦;融洽 _____

A Listen to the passage and fill in the blanks. 🎧 40

Martin Luther _____, Jr. was a great leader.

He _____ _____ in the American South in the middle of the 1900s.

He was a black man.

At that time, many Americans treated blacks very _____.

Dr. King believed that all people should have the _____ to be treated the same.

He _____ for all people to live together in peace.

He led _____ and gave speeches.

He was arrested many times, but he never _____ _____.

He believed in _____.

In 1964, he won the Nobel Peace _____.

That same year, the United States _____ the Civil Rights Act.

It changed the laws that were _____ to African-Americans.

It _____ equal rights to all Americans.

To honor him, Martin Luther King, Jr. Day is _____ in January every year.

B Write the meaning of each word or phrase from Word List in English.

1 成長　　　_____

2 貧窮地　　_____

3 權利　　　_____

4 夢想；理想　_____

5 和平　　　_____

6 遊行抗議　_____

7 演說；演講　_____

8 逮捕；拘留　_____

9 放棄；讓出　_____

10 非暴力　　_____

11 贏得；獲得　_____

12 通過　　　_____

13 不公平的　_____

14 保證　　　_____

15 尊敬；敬重　_____

16 慶祝　　　_____

05 Many Jobs

Listen to the passage and fill in the blanks. 🎧 41

Many people have _____.

A job is the _____ that people do.

Most people work at a job to _____ money.

They usually get paid hourly, weekly, or _____.

With that money, they can take care of _____ and their families.

There are many _____ of jobs.

Some workers earn money by growing or making _____.

Farmers _____ the food we eat every day.

Workers at factories produce many _____ we use every day.

Some workers earn money by having _____ jobs.

These are jobs like waiter, cook, _____ person, and salesperson.

Workers with these jobs provide services for _____.

Others have _____ jobs.

Professional jobs _____ special education and training.

Some of these jobs are doctor, lawyer, _____, and artist.

B Write the meaning of each word or phrase from Word List in English.

1	職業；工作	_____	8	製造；生產	_____
2	賺錢；掙錢	_____	9	工廠	_____
3	支薪	_____	10	產物；產品	_____
4	每小時	_____	11	服務	_____
5	每週	_____	12	專門職業的	_____
6	每月	_____	13	需要	_____
7	商品；貨物	_____	14	工程師	_____

06 Volunteers and Community Jobs

A Listen to the passage and fill in the blanks. 🎧 42

Some people do not earn _____ for their work.

They work for _____ and help others.

We call them _____.

Volunteers do many _____ jobs.

Some people volunteer at _____.

They assist doctors and nurses in taking care of _____.

Other people work at _____ shelters or food banks.

They help take care of more _____ people.

Volunteers also help when people are _____ _____ because of earthquakes or floods.

There are also special jobs that help the _____ community.

These are community jobs such as _____ and police officer.

They _____ _____ the whole community and get paid by the community.

All of these volunteers and community jobs are _____ our communities.

They make our communities _____ places.

B Write the meaning of each word or phrase from Word List in English.

1 免費 _____
2 志工 _____
3 醫院 _____
4 協助……做…… _____
5 照顧 _____
6 病患;病人 _____
7 無家可歸的 _____
8 遊民收容所 _____
9 食物銀行 _____
10 不幸的 _____
11 陷入了麻煩 _____
12 地震 _____
13 洪水;水災 _____
14 專門的 _____
15 全部;全體 _____
16 消防員 _____
17 警察 _____
18 改善;改進 _____

07 What Is a Map?

A map is a _____ of a place.

It looks like a _____ from above.

It might show cities, states, or _____.

It might show a small neighborhood or the _____ world.

Maps can be very _____.

Mostly, we use them to find _____.

We also use them to show how far one _____ is from another.

Most maps have _____ on them.

A symbol is a picture that stands for a _____ _____ on a map.

There could be symbols for houses, buildings, rivers, _____, streets, and more.

Maps have a _____ _____.

A map key explains what the symbols on a map _____.

Maps also have _____.

The title tells you what the map _____.

These map _____ help us read and use the maps.

B Write the meaning of each word or phrase from Word List in English.

1	地圖	_____	8	位置；場所	_____
2	繪畫；描畫	_____	9	符號；記號	_____
3	看起來像	_____	10	代表……	_____
4	視域；視野	_____	11	真實的	_____
5	鄰近地區	_____	12	地圖索引	_____
6	全部的	_____	13	標題；題目	_____
7	有用的	_____	14	特徵；特色	_____

Daily Test 08 Maps and Directions

A Listen to the passage and fill in the blanks. 🎧 44

Before we can use a map, we need to _____ a few things about it.

First, we should find the _____ _____.

The compass rose shows the four main _____ on a map.

It _____ _____ which directions are north, south, east, and west.

On most maps, north is straight up on the map and is _____ with an "N."

East is to the right, south is _____ down, and west is to the left.

Maps also have a _____.

All maps are _____ than the real area that they show.

The map scale lets you calculate the real _____ between two points.

For example, the scale on one map may be that one _____

represents ten kilometers.

On this map, two cities are three centimeters _____ from each other.

In reality, thirty kilometers is the distance _____ the two cities.

B Write the meaning of each word or phrase from Word List in English.

1 幾個；有一些 _____
2 發現；找出 _____
3 羅盤玫瑰 _____
4 主要的 _____
5 方向；方位 _____
6 指出 _____
7 正上方 _____
8 用……做記號 _____
9 正下方 _____
10 地圖比例尺 _____
11 計算；估算 _____
12 距離 _____
13 表示；象徵 _____
14 遠離 _____

09 Natural Resources

Natural _____ are useful things that come from nature.

Nature is full of resources that are _____ for people to use.

Land, water, and air are some important _____ resources.

We use natural resources for food and _____.

We need water to drink and air to _____.

We need land and _____ to grow food.

_____, oil, and natural gas are used to make energy.

This energy lets us drive our cars and make _____ for our homes.

We also make many _____ from natural resources.

We can use cotton and _____ from animals to make clothes.

We use trees to build our homes and to make many things we use

_____ _____.

Rocks can be used to build _____ and buildings.

B Write the meaning of each word or phrase from Word List in English.

1	自然的	_____	8	能源；能量	_____
2	資源	_____	9	呼吸；吸入	_____
3	天然資源	_____	10	煤	_____
4	有用的	_____	11	駕駛	_____
5	自然；自然界	_____	12	電；電流	_____
6	充滿……的	_____	13	棉花	_____
7	現成的	_____	14	羊毛	_____

10 Caring for Our Resources

A Listen to the passage and fill in the blanks.   🎧 46

We _____ natural resources every day.

So we have to be careful not to _____ _____ all of them.

If we do not _____ our natural resources, we might not have

_____ _____ them in the future.

One way to _____ resources is to reuse them.

_____ paper, bags, and boxes as much as you can.

Another way to save resources is to use _____ _____ them.

Try to reduce the _____ _____ resources you use.

You can _____ _____ the lights when you leave a room.

You can turn the water off when you _____ your teeth.

You can also recycle some _____.

To recycle means to make a new thing from an _____ _____.

Collect the used items and put them into the _____ _____.

When we _____ something, we can use it again and again.

B Write the meaning of each word or phrase from Word List in English.

1 仔細的 _____

2 用完;耗盡 _____

3 節省 _____

4 將來 _____

5 保存;保護 _____

6 重複利用 _____

7 像……那樣多 _____

8 減少使用 _____

9 減少;降低 _____

10 ……的總量 _____

11 關掉 _____

12 刷牙 _____

13 回收;再利用 _____

14 集中;收集 _____

15 項目;品目 _____

16 將……放入…… _____

17 資源回收筒 _____

18 一再地 _____

11 Native Americans

A Listen to the passage and fill in the blanks. 🎧 47

Native Americans were the _____ people to live in America.

They are also called American _____.

The _____ of the Native Americans were people from Asia.

As the years passed, these people formed their own _____.

They had their own languages and _____.

Some tribes _____ for their food.

Other tribes _____ food such as corn and beans.

Native Americans lived in different _____ of homes.

The Lakota lived in tepees like _____.

The Pueblo lived in _____ houses.

The Iroquois lived in _____.

Native Americans made the things they _____ and wore.

They made canoes, baskets, pottery, and many other _____.

Today, Native Americans still live in all _____ _____ the United States.

They carry on the _____ of their ancestors.

B Write the meaning of each word or phrase from Word List in English.

1	美國原住民	_____	10	美國拉科塔族	_____
2	祖宗；祖先	_____	11	圓錐形帳篷	_____
3	相傳	_____	12	美國普韋布洛族	_____
4	組織；成立	_____	13	曬乾的泥磚	_____
5	某人的	_____	14	美國依洛郭亦族	_____
6	部落；種族	_____	15	長形房屋	_____
7	語言	_____	16	陶器	_____
8	習慣；風俗	_____	17	手工藝品	_____
9	生長；成長	_____	18	繼續；進行	_____

12 Early American Empires

Listen to the passage and fill in the blanks.　　　　　🎧 48

There were many tribes in the _____.

Some of them _____ their own empires.

The three great American _____ were the Maya, Aztec, and Inca.

The Mayans lived in the _____ of Central America.

They built great cities with _____ and palaces.

Their _____ was very developed.

The Mayans knew _____ _____ write.

They also had _____ math and building skills.

Like other ancient people, the Mayans _____ many nature gods.

The Aztecs lived in the area of _____ Mexico.

They built their city on _____ in a lake.

The Aztecs were very _____.

They _____ many people around them.

They built huge stone _____ devoted to their sun god.

The Incas lived in the _____ Mountains in South America.

Their _____, like Machu Picchu, were high in the mountains.

The Incas built _____ stone walls.

B Write the meaning of each word or phrase from Word List in English.

1	美洲	_____	9	古代的	_____
2	建立；設立	_____	10	崇拜；敬仰	_____
3	帝國	_____	11	自然神	_____
4	瑪雅族	_____	12	阿茲提克人	_____
5	神殿；聖堂	_____	13	現代的	_____
6	皇宮；宮殿	_____	14	好戰的	_____
7	文明	_____	15	將……奉獻給	_____
8	先進的	_____	16	不可思議的	_____

13 What Are Living Things?

A Listen to the passage and fill in the blanks. 🎧49

Everything on Earth is _____ living or nonliving.

Animals and plants are _____ _____.

Living things _____ food, water, and air to live.

Living things grow and _____.

They can also make new living things like _____.

Water, air, and rocks are _____ things.

Nonliving things do not need food, water, or _____.

Nonliving things do not _____ or change.

They cannot make new things _____ themselves.

Living things must have _____.

Shelter is a _____ place to live.

Shelter protects them from their _____ and from other animals.

Living things also must have room to grow or to _____ _____.

Some living things, such as _____, need very little space.

Other living things, such as elephants, may need a lot of _____.

B Write the meaning of each word or phrase from Word List in English.

1 或;任一的 _____

2 有生命的 _____

3 無生命的 _____

4 非生物 _____

5 生物 _____

6 躲避處 _____

7 安全的 _____

8 保護 _____

9 環境 _____

10 空間;場所 _____

11 到處移動 _____

12 空間 _____

14 How Do Living Things Survive in the Cold?

A Listen to the passage and fill in the blanks. 🎧 50

The coldest place on Earth is _____.

The temperature there is always below _____.

But many animals _____ live there.

How do they manage to _____ in such cold weather?

These animals have _____ their bodies to the cold.

Seals and whales in Antarctica have many _____ of fat.

This fat helps keep their _____ warm.

Penguins stay warm because they have small and thick _____.

Some plants and animals live in the _____ tundra.

Many tundra animals have thick _____ to keep them warm.

Plants do not grow very _____ there.

They grow in _____ close to the ground.

This protects them from the cold and the _____.

What about _____?

Clothing helps people _____ _____ the same way animals' fur does.

B Write the meaning of each word or phrase from Word List in English.

1 南極洲 _____
2 溫度；氣溫 _____
3 溫度；氣溫 _____
4 還；仍舊 _____
5 達成；設法 _____
6 活下來；倖存 _____
7 使適應 _____
8 層 _____
9 脂肪 _____
10 保持暖和 _____
11 羽毛 _____
12 北極的 _____
13 凍土地帶 _____
14 毛皮 _____
15 人類 _____
16 衣服；衣著 _____

15 How Do Plants Grow and Change?

A Listen to the passage and fill in the blanks.

Every living thing has a _____ _____.

A life cycle shows how a living thing grows, lives, and _____.

A plant's life cycle _____ with a seed.

When a seed gets water and nutrients from the soil, it starts to _____.

Then, the seed _____ and grows into an adult plant.

Again, the adult plant makes _____, and a new life cycle begins.

The life cycle of a _____ plant

Let's look _____ at the life cycle of a bean plant.

1. A bean seed is planted and _____ in the ground.

2. After _____ a week, the seed germinates. The roots grow _____.

3. Then, one week later, the bean plant sprouts and becomes a _____.

4. After six weeks, the bean plant becomes _____ _____.

5. Flowers grow and get _____. They make bean seeds.

B Write the meaning of each word or phrase from Word List in English.

1	生命週期	_____	8	碗豆	_____
2	種子；籽	_____	9	緊密地	_____
3	營養物	_____	10	植物；苗	_____
4	土；泥土	_____	11	灌溉	_____
5	發芽；生長	_____	12	變短；縮小	_____
6	芽；新芽	_____	13	幼苗；秧苗	_____
7	成長為	_____	14	使肥沃	_____

16 How Do Plants Survive in the Desert?

A Listen to the passage and fill in the blanks. 🎧 52

Plants live almost _____.

Some plants _____ live in the desert.

Deserts have very _____ environments.

_____ are very hot and dry with little rain.

Few kinds of plants and animals have _____ to living there.

However, some plants, like the cactus, grow well in the _____.

How do they manage to survive in such dry _____?

A cactus has a thick stem and _____ leaves.

The stems and leaves help the cactus _____ water inside it.

Then, it can use the water _____ when it needs it.

So, it can grow for a long time _____ any rain at all.

A cactus's roots _____ _____ away from it.

The _____ are also very close to the ground.

This lets the roots _____ large amounts of water when it rains.

B Write the meaning of each word or phrase from Word List in English.

1	到處	_____	7	仙人掌	_____
2	甚至	_____	8	多刺的	_____
3	沙漠；荒野	_____	9	儲存；儲藏	_____
4	嚴酷的	_____	10	無；沒有	_____
5	少；不多的	_____	11	攤開；散開	_____
6	很少數的	_____	12	捕捉；奪取	_____

17 Kinds of Animals

What do a cat, a lion, and a dolphin have in _____?

They are all _____.

A mammal is an animal with _____ or hair.

Most mammals give birth to live _____.

Mammals _____ their young with milk from their mothers.

A bird is an animal that has a _____, feathers, wings, and legs.

Most birds can fly _____ their wings.

Birds lay _____. Chicks _____ from the eggs.

Ducks, peacocks, and _____ are all birds.

A reptile is an animal that has dry skin covered with _____.

Most _____ lay eggs and walk on four legs.

Snakes, turtles, and _____ are all reptiles.

An _____ is an animal that lives on land and in water.

Most amphibians have _____, wet skin and lay eggs.

Frogs and _____ are amphibians.

Fish live _____ water.

Most fish have scales, _____, and gills.

They _____ eggs.

Angelfish and _____ are fish.

B Write the meaning of each word or phrase from Word List in English.

1 共同的 _____
2 哺乳動物 _____
3 生（孩子） _____
4 幼小動物 _____
5 哺乳；餵 _____
6 鳥 _____
7 鳥嘴；喙 _____
8 產卵；生蛋 _____
9 孵出 _____
10 爬蟲類 _____
11 被……覆蓋 _____
12 鱗；殼 _____
13 鱷魚 _____
14 兩棲動物 _____
15 蠑螈 _____
16 鰭 _____
17 扁鮫；神仙魚 _____
18 鯊魚 _____

18 Insects

A Listen to the passage and fill in the blanks. 🎧54

There are millions of _____ of insects.

Insects include ants, butterflies, bees, and _____.

Many look different from one _____.

But insects all have many _____.

All insects have three _____ _____ and six legs.

Most _____ lay eggs.

Let's take a closer _____ _____ the three main body parts: the head,

thorax, and abdomen.

The _____ has the insect's eyes, antennae, and mouth.

Insects use their _____ to feel things.

The _____ has the insect's legs and wings.

All insects have three _____ of legs.

Not all of them have wings _____.

The _____ is usually the largest part.

_____ insects lay eggs from their abdomen.

Insects like bees have their _____ there.

B Write the meaning of each word or phrase from Word List in English.

1	百萬的	_____	8	（昆蟲的）胸部	_____
2	物種；種類	_____	9	腹部	_____
3	昆蟲	_____	10	觸角；觸鬚	_____
4	蝴蝶	_____	11	一雙；一對	_____
5	蟋蟀	_____	12	可是；然而	_____
6	類似；相似	_____	13	女性的	_____
7	身體的部分	_____	14	（昆蟲的）螫針	_____

19 The Life Cycle of an Animal

A Listen to the passage and fill in the blanks. 🎧 55

How do animals grow and _____?

All animals have a _____ _____.

A life cycle is all of the _____ that animals go through during their lives.

Most animals _____ _____ four stages: birth, growth, reproduction, and _____.

When mammals are born, they are _____.

They cannot see or _____.

Their mothers must take care of them until they can _____ _____ of themselves.

As mammals grow up, they start to look like their _____.

For cats and dogs, it _____ about a year to become an adult.

For humans, it takes more than ten years to _____.

When mammals become adults, they can _____.

Then they can have their _____ young like themselves.

Finally, the last stage is _____.

When mammals _____ the end of their lives, they die.

B Write the meaning of each word or phrase from Word List in English.

1 生命週期 _____
2 階段；舞台 _____
3 經歷 _____
4 分娩；出生 _____
5 生長；成長 _____
6 繁育 _____
7 死；死亡 _____
8 無助的 _____
9 照顧 _____

10 成長 _____
11 看起來像…… _____
12 雙親 _____
13 需要；花費 _____
14 成年人 _____
15 成熟的 _____
16 生殖 _____
17 最後；終於 _____
18 到達；達到 _____

20 The Life Cycle of a Frog

A **Listen to the passage and fill in the blanks.** 🎧56

Frogs are _____.

So their life cycles are _____ from mammals.

In fact, frogs have very _____ life cycles.

Frogs lay eggs in water in _____.

After about two weeks, _____ hatch from the eggs.

Tadpoles actually do not _____ frogs at all.

They do not have any legs but have _____.

Tadpoles also have _____.

Their gills let them _____ and live in the water.

As tadpoles grow older, they get ready to live _____ _____.

They _____ legs, and their tails become shorter.

Also, they develop lungs, _____ let them breathe air on land.

Then, the tadpoles start to look more like _____.

After about _____ weeks, the frogs have become adults and have no tails.

They move onto land and live there most of their _____.

B **Write the meaning of each word or phrase from Word List in English.**

1 青蛙 _____
2 事實上 _____
3 獨一無二的 _____
4 蝌蚪 _____
5 像；類似 _____
6 一點也不…… _____
7 尾巴；尾部 _____
8 （魚）鰓 _____
9 呼吸；呼氣 _____
10 變得更年長 _____
11 準備好 _____
12 在陸地上 _____
13 發展；發育 _____
14 變成；成為 _____
15 肺 _____
16 到……上 _____
17 大多數 _____
18 生活；生命 _____

21

21 What Are Food Chains?

A Listen to the passage and fill in the blanks. 🎧 57

All animals need _____ to live.

Food _____ them energy to survive.

Different animals eat different _____.

Some eat plants. Some eat other _____.

A food chain shows the _____ in which animals eat plants and other animals.

At the bottom of the _____ _____ are plants.

The sun gives plants _____.

Animals that eat plants are the next _____.

We call them _____ _____.

They are usually small insects like _____.

Animals like _____ and rabbits are also plant eaters.

Animals that eat other animals are the _____ link.

We call them _____ _____.

They might be small animals like frogs and _____.

Then, _____ animals like hawks and bears eat these small animals.

Animals that are not _____ by other animals are at the top of the food chain. Actually, people are _____ _____ _____ of many food chains.

B Write the meaning of each word or phrase from Word List in English.

1	食物鏈	_____	7	松鼠	_____
2	順序；次序	_____	8	食肉性動物	_____
3	在……底部	_____	9	鷹	_____
4	（鏈狀物的）環	_____	10	追獵	_____
5	草食性動物	_____	11	被……追捕	_____
6	蚱蜢	_____	12	在……頂端	_____

22 The Ocean Food Chain

A Listen to the passage and fill in the blanks. 🎧 58

Food chains also _____ in the oceans.

The _____ are full of life.

These life forms all either eat or get eaten by _____ on the

food chain.

_____ are the lowest on the ocean food chain.

They are plants that make food from the sun's _____.

Small creatures, such as _____, consume the algae.

Then, _____ bigger creatures eat the plankton.

These are often _____ like clams, shrimp, and crabs.

Then, small _____ eat the shellfish.

Some small fish are cod, _____, and flatfish.

Next, _____ fish eat the small fish.

Some large fish are tuna, swordfish, and _____.

Finally, animals like _____ _____ and great white sharks eat the

large fish.

They are at the top of the _____ _____.

B Write the meaning of each word or phrase from Word List in English.

1	存在	_____	11	蛤蜊	_____
2	海洋；海	_____	12	蝦	_____
3	生命形式	_____	13	蟹	_____
4	被……吃	_____	14	鱈魚	_____
5	生物；動物	_____	15	鯖	_____
6	水藻；海藻	_____	16	比目魚	_____
7	浮游生物	_____	17	鮪魚	_____
8	消耗；花費	_____	18	劍魚	_____
9	輕微地	_____	19	殺人鯨	_____
10	有殼的水生動物	_____	20	大白鯊	_____

23 What Is the Solar System?

🎧 59

A Listen to the passage and fill in the blanks.

We all live on _____.

Earth is part of a larger system called _____ _____ _____.

The solar system is _____ _____ _____ the sun and the planets.

A planet is a huge _____ that moves around the sun.

There are eight _____ in the solar system.

Earth is one of eight planets that _____ the sun.

In order of the planets from the sun, they are: _____, Venus, Earth, Mars,

Jupiter, Saturn, _____, and Neptune.

The sun is the _____ of the solar system.

The eight planets move in _____ around the sun.

Each path is _____ an orbit.

The planets are different from _____ _____.

Some are _____ than Earth. _____ are larger.

They look different, and they are at different _____ from the sun.

B Write the meaning of each word or phrase from Word List in English.

1	太陽系	_____	10	地球	_____
2	由……構成	_____	11	火星	_____
3	行星	_____	12	木星	_____
4	物體;物件	_____	13	土星	_____
5	繞著……轉	_____	14	天王星	_____
6	運行軌道	_____	15	海王星	_____
7	依……順序	_____	16	路線;軌道	_____
8	水星	_____	17	被稱為……	_____
9	金星	_____	18	距離;路程	_____

24 What Causes the Seasons?

A Listen to the passage and fill in the blanks. 🎧 60

There are four different _____ in a year: spring, summer,

_____, and winter.

All _____ the year, the seasons change.

So what _____ them to change?

Earth moves around the sun while it _____ each day.

It takes Earth one year to complete a _____ _____ around the sun.

Earth is always _____ in the same direction.

As Earth orbits the sun, the part that is tilted _____ the sun changes.

This _____ the four seasons.

When the part of Earth where you live is tilted toward the sun, the sun's rays

_____ hit that part of Earth.

So it is _____.

When the part of Earth where you live is tilted _____ from the sun,

it is winter.

The same _____ repeats each year.

B Write the meaning of each word or phrase from Word List in English.

1	季節	_____	8	傾斜的	_____
2	遍及;遍布	_____	9	方向;方位	_____
3	導致;使發生	_____	10	向;朝	_____
4	當……的時候	_____	11	太陽光	_____
5	旋轉;轉動	_____	12	直接地	_____
6	完成;結束	_____	13	遠離	_____
7	傾斜;偏斜	_____	14	重複;重做	_____

25 Addition and Subtraction

A Listen to the passage and fill in the blanks. 🎧 61

Addition is _____ two or more numbers together.

Suppose there are 3 _____ on a leaf. Then, 4 more ants _____ them.

How many ants are _____ now?

       3 + 4 _____ 7

There are _____ ants.

The _____ you get after you add numbers is called the *sum*.

So, you can say, "The _____ of 3 + 4 is 7."

Or, you can say, "Three _____ four equals seven."

_____ is taking a number away from another one.

Suppose your friend has 5 _____.

You are hungry, so you _____ 2 cookies.

How many cookies are _____ now?

    _____ − 2 = 3

There are _____ cookies left.

The number you have left after you _____ is called the *difference*.

So, you can say, "The _____ of 5 − 2 is 3."

Or, you can say, "Five minus two _____ three."

B Write the meaning of each word or phrase from Word List in English.

1	加法	_____	8	減；減算	_____
2	將……相加	_____	9	帶走；拿走	_____
3	假定	_____	10	拿；取	_____
4	參加	_____	11	剩下	_____
5	總和	_____	12	減；減去	_____
6	加；加上	_____	13	差額	_____
7	等於	_____	14	減；減去	_____

A Listen to the passage and fill in the blanks. 🎧 62

We use _____ to buy things.

Money can be both _____ and paper bills.

All bills and coins have different _____.

There are several kinds of coins and _____ in American money.

A penny is _____ one cent. 1 penny = 1¢

A _____ is worth five cents. 1 nickel = 5¢

A _____ is worth ten cents. 1 dime = 10¢

A _____ is worth twenty-five cents. 1 quarter = 25¢

A half-dollar is worth fifty _____. 1 half-dollar = 50¢

And the value of a one-dollar coin is one _____ cents.

1 dollar = 100¢

There are also bills for the _____ values of money:

$1, $2, $5, $10, $20, _____, and $100.

We often write money _____ like this: $1.50.

For $1.50, we can say, "one _____ and fifty cents."

So $25.20 is "twenty-five dollars and _____ cents."

B Write the meaning of each word or phrase from Word List in English.

1 硬幣；錢幣 _____

2 （紙）鈔票 _____

3 價值；價格 _____

4 幾個的 _____

5 一分錢 _____

6 有……的價值 _____

7 一分值的硬幣 _____

8 五分錢 _____

9 十分錢 _____

10 25分錢 _____

11 半毛錢 _____

12 下面的 _____

27 Telling Time

A Listen to the passage and fill in the blanks. 🎧 63

_____ usually have two hands: a short hand and a long hand.

The short hand _____ the hour.

So, it is also called the _____ _____.

The long hand shows the minute.

So, it is also called the _____ _____.

How do we say the _____?

It's easy. Just _____ the hour and then the minute.

So 2:10 is "two _____."

And 5:25 is "five _____."

Sometimes, the time may be 4:_____.

We can say either "four thirty" or "_____ past four."

Also, for 7:15, we can say "seven fifteen" or "15 minutes _____ seven."

And for 9:45, we can say "nine forty-five" or "15 minutes _____ ten."

When the long hand is on the _____ and the short hand is on the 6,

then the time is _____. We can write it 6:00.

6:00 means the _____ _____ 6 o'clock.

B Write the meaning of each word or phrase from Word List in English.

1 時鐘 _____
2 短針 _____
3 長針 _____
4 小時 _____
5 時針 _____

6 分鐘 _____
7 分針 _____
8 半；一半 _____
9 ……點鐘 _____
10 與……相同 _____

A Listen to the passage and fill in the blanks. ∩ 64

We can _____ time with a calendar or a clock.

A calendar shows time in days, weeks, and _____.

Take a look at a _____.

On the first page, it shows _____.

January is the _____ month of the year.

There are _____ months in 1 year.

They are January, _____, March, April, May, June, July, August,

September, _____, November, and December.

So your calendar has a _____ of twelve pages.

On each page, there are four or five _____ with numbers on them.

Each number _____ a day of the month.

There are 7 _____ in 1 week.

They are Sunday, Monday, Tuesday, Wednesday, _____, Friday, and

Saturday.

Each row represents 1 _____.

Every month has _____ 4 weeks.

B Write the meaning of each word or phrase from Word List in English.

1	量；測量	_____	11	五月	_____
2	日曆	_____	12	六月	_____
3	天	_____	13	七月	_____
4	星期	_____	14	八月	_____
5	月	_____	15	九月	_____
6	看一看	_____	16	十月	_____
7	一月	_____	17	十一月	_____
8	二月	_____	18	十二月	_____
9	三月	_____	19	列；排	_____
10	四月	_____	20	代表	_____

29 Parts of Speech

🎧 65

A Listen to the passage and fill in the blanks.

Every _____ has a subject and a verb.

    Tom runs fast.   She eats _____.

In the sentences above, *Tom* and *She* are _____, and *runs* and *eats* are verbs.

The subject is usually a _____.

A noun names a _____, place, or thing.

A verb _____ the action in a sentence.

Sing, *dance*, *smile*, and *laugh* are all _____.

Nouns and verbs are the most important _____ _____ _____ in a sentence.

We _____ use other parts of speech.

Pronouns are _____ like *I*, *he*, *she*, *it*, *we*, *you*, and *they*.

We use _____ in place of nouns.

_____ are words that describe nouns and pronouns.

    a pretty dog   a _____ boy   a happy cat

Pretty, *tall*, and *happy* are _____ adjectives.

_____ describe verbs.

    He cried _____.   She walks slowly.

_____ often help us with location.

They are words like *in*, *on*, *under*, _____, and *by*.

B Write the meaning of each word or phrase from Word List in English.

1	句子	_____	8	詞類	_____
2	主題；題目	_____	9	代名詞	_____
3	動詞	_____	10	代替	_____
4	名詞	_____	11	形容詞	_____
5	名字；姓名	_____	12	副詞	_____
6	描寫；描繪	_____	13	突然地	_____
7	行動；行為	_____	14	介係詞	_____

30 Contractions and Abbreviations

A Listen to the passage and fill in the blanks. ∩ 66

When we write, we sometimes _____ two words to make one shorter word.

The shorter word is called a _____.

We put an _____ (') between two words when we make a contraction.

I am = I'm	you are = you're	it is = _____
do not = don't	cannot = can't	is not = _____

Some words can be _____ or abbreviated.

Many abbreviations begin with a capital letter and end with a _____.

The days of the week are often _____.

Monday = Mon.	_____ = Tue.	Wednesday = Wed.
Thursday = Thur.	Friday = Fri.	_____ = Sat.
Sunday = Sun.		

The _____ of the year are often abbreviated.

January = Jan.	_____ = Feb.	March = Mar.
April = Apr.	_____ = Aug.	September = Sept.
October = Oct.	November = Nov.	_____ = Dec.

The months May, June, and _____ are not abbreviated.

People's _____ and types of streets are also often abbreviated.

Mister = Mr.	_____ = Prof.	Doctor = Dr.
Street = St.	_____ = Ave.	Road = Rd.

B Write the meaning of each word or phrase from Word List in English.

1 結合；聯合 _____

2 縮短；縮約 _____

3 省略符號 _____

4 使變短；縮短 _____

5 縮寫；省略 _____

6 縮寫字 _____

7 大寫字母 _____

8 句號 _____

9 標題；題目 _____

10 類型；型式 _____

11 教授 _____

12 街；街道 _____

13 大街；大道 _____

14 公路；路 _____

31 Types of Writing

There are many different types of _____.

Can you name _____ _____ them?

A _____ is a short writing that uses rhymes.

Poems often repeat regular _____, like *cold* and *hold*, at the ends of lines.

A fairy tale is a story for children in which _____ things happen.

A short story that teaches a _____ lesson is called a fable.

Animals talk and act like people in many _____.

A _____ is a long story of fiction.

Novels often have many _____ in them.

A _____ is a true story of a person's life.

An _____ is a biography written by the person himself.

Fiction means stories that did not actually happen, such as _____ or novels.

When you make up a story, you are creating _____.

Nonfiction is writing that is about _____ or actual events.

A biography and autobiography are _____.

1	詩	_____	9	（長篇）小說 _____
2	韻；韻腳	_____	10	（總稱）小說 _____
3	有規則的	_____	11	傳記 _____
4	童話	_____	12	自傳 _____
5	有魔力的	_____	13	虛構；編造 _____
6	寓意	_____	14	非小說 _____
7	教訓；課程	_____	15	事實 _____
8	寓言	_____	16	真實事件 _____

32 The Emperor's New Clothes

A Listen to the passage and fill in the blanks.　　　　🎧68

A long time ago, there lived an _____ who loved clothes.

Every day, he wore the finest clothes and _____ _____ his clothes.

One day, two _____ arrived in town. They told the emperor they could make the most beautiful _____ in the world.

"We are _____ _____ make magic cloth. Only smart people can see it," they said.

The emperor gave them a lot of money and told them to _____ the magic cloth.

Day and night, they _____ to weave cloth. But they had nothing at all on their _____.

The emperor _____ _____ the room to see the cloth. But he couldn't see ___ _____.

"This is _____. Am I stupid?" he thought.

But out loud he said, "It looks _____!"

At last, the day came for the emperor to wear his new clothes _____ _____.

The emperor walked very _____ in his underclothes! The people on the streets _____ and called out, "The _____ are beautiful."

No one would _____ he could not see anything. Then, a little child in the _____ cried out,

"He isn't _____ any clothes!"

B Write the meaning of each word or phrase from Word List in English.

1 皇帝；國王 _____

2 衣著；衣服 _____

3 穿著 _____

4 漂亮的 _____

5 炫耀 _____

6 賊；小偷 _____

7 能夠 _____

8 魔法的 _____

9 布匹；織物 _____

10 織；編 _____

11 假裝；裝作 _____

12 織布機 _____

13 可怕的 _____

14 非凡的 _____

15 內衣；襯衣 _____

16 大聲喊出 _____

17 承認；准許 _____

18 人群 _____

33 A World of Colors

Look all _____ you.

You can see many different _____.

Some of them are _____. Others are dark.

All of these colors come from three _____ colors.

The three primary colors are red, _____, and blue.

With _____ three primary colors, we can make other colors.

How can we do _____?

We simply mix two primary colors _____.

We can _____ red and yellow to get orange.

We can mix red and blue to get _____.

And we can combine blue and yellow to _____ green.

Orange, purple, and green are the three _____ colors.

In painting, primary and secondary colors are very _____.

By combining different _____ of them, we can make any color in the world.

B Write the meaning of each word or phrase from Word List in English.

1	環顧	_____	6	結合；聯合 _____
2	基本的	_____	7	第二的 _____
3	原色	_____	8	第二次色 _____
4	混合；混入	_____	9	繪畫 _____
5	紫色	_____	10	數量 _____

Daily Test 34 Lines and Shapes

Listen to the passage and fill in the blanks. 🎧70

We often use lines when we _____.

_____ come in all types: straight, curved, zigzag, wavy, and spiral.

———— straight line   ⌒ curved line   ⧢ _____ line

〰 wavy line   ◉ _____ line

Lines can be fine or _____, too.

———— fine line   ━━ rough line

A line that _____ _____ and down is called a vertical line.

A line that goes from left to right is called a _____ line.

A line that moves up or down at _____ _____ is called a diagonal line.

| vertical line   ——— horizontal line   / _____ line

Can you see the _____?

When lines join together, they make _____.

There are three basic shapes: squares, circles, and _____.

A square is _____ _____ four straight lines. □

A circle is formed by a single _____ line. ○

And a triangle is formed by three _____ lines. △

Write the meaning of each word or phrase from Word List in English.

1 線條 _____
2 畫；繪製 _____
3 平直的 _____
4 彎曲的 _____
5 曲折的 _____
6 波浪形的 _____
7 螺旋形的 _____
8 纖細的 _____
9 粗糙的 _____
10 垂直的 _____
11 水平的 _____
12 對角線的 _____
13 形成；構成 _____
14 由……形成 _____

35

35 Musicians and Their Instruments

There are many kinds of _____.

They all belong to different _____.

There are _____, string, keyboard, woodwind, and brass instruments.

In an orchestra, _____ play all of these instruments.

The _____ is a percussion instrument.

A _____ plays a drum.

Violins, cellos, and _____ are three stringed instruments.

Violinists, _____, and guitarists play them.

The piano and organ are the two most common _____ instruments.

They are played by pianists and _____.

Flutes and _____ are two woodwinds.

_____ and clarinetists play these instruments.

Trumpets and _____ are two kinds of brass instruments.

A _____ plays the trumpet.

And a _____ plays the trombone.

Together, all of these musicians can make _____ music.

Ⓑ Write the meaning of each word or phrase from Word List in English.

1	樂器	_____	11 小提琴手	_____
2	屬於	_____	12 大提琴手	_____
3	打擊（樂器）	_____	13 吉他手	_____
4	弦（樂器）	_____	14 普遍的	_____
5	鍵盤（樂器）	_____	15 鋼琴家	_____
6	木管（樂器）	_____	16 風琴手	_____
7	銅管（樂器）	_____	17 長笛手	_____
8	音樂家	_____	18 黑管手	_____
9	鼓手	_____	19 小號手	_____
10	有弦的	_____	20 長號手	_____

36 Mozart and Beethoven

A Listen to the passage and fill in the blanks. ○ 72

Composers write, or compose, _____.

Wolfgang Amadeus Mozart was one of the world's _____ composers.

He was a child _____.

He played the piano and _____ music from a young age.

Mozart _____ all over Europe.

He wrote many _____ pieces of music.

He composed operas, symphonies, _____, and many other pieces.

Sadly, he died when he was only _____ years old.

Ludwig van _____ was another great composer.

Like Mozart, he also _____ to play music.

But he soon _____ down in Vienna.

He was an _____ pianist.

But he started going _____ when he was around 30.

Still, he _____ to play and compose music.

His *Ninth Symphony* is one of the world's most _____ pieces of music.

Today, people _____ listen to Mozart's and Beethoven's music.

B Write the meaning of each word or phrase from Word List in English.

1	作曲家	_____	7	傑出的	_____
2	作曲	_____	8	交響曲	_____
3	譜曲	_____	9	彌撒曲	_____
4	偉大的	_____	10	定居下來	_____
5	天才	_____	11	優秀的	_____
6	旅行	_____	12	變聾	_____

MEMO